THE PACT

KEITH DISSINGER

Publisher's Note: This is a work of fiction. Names, characters, places, and incidents are a product of the author's imagination. Locales and public names are sometimes used for atmospheric purposes. Any resemblance to actual people, living or dead, or to businesses, companies, events, institutions, or locales is completely coincidental.

THE PACT / KEITH DISSINGER
1st paperback edition 2017
Formatting by Frostbite Publishing

Chapter One

Twenty miles off the coast of Florida, the small, hand built raft was sinking slowly. An old man and a young girl lay sprawled across the sodden wooden surface. Their minds dulled from the days at sea, they did not notice or seem to care about the raft riding lower and lower on the blue waters of the sea.

The passage from Cuba had so far taken five days. Their stores of rice and bread had run out two days ago, and they had finished the fresh water the day before. Open sores and rashes, caused by being constantly wet, covered their bodies. Salt from the sea dried and caked around their eyes, in the corner of their mouths, and under their arms causing painful chafing. There was no shade, and the merciless sun beat down upon their sun burned skin.

The eight-foot by ten-foot raft consisted of old wooden planking lashed to empty fifty-five gallon drums. A storm had destroyed the homemade mast and sail some time ago. It rode low on the waves now. Many of the lashings were frayed and beginning to come apart. The plank deck was flush with the surface of the sea. Growing swells washed across the deck of the raft and her helpless passengers.

Dannillo Hetes covered his eyes with his arm to block the sharp sunshine as the ocean raised, then lowered the failing raft. He lay across the waterlogged deck beside his twelve-year-old granddaughter Lolita. He felt lethargic and silently prayed for an end to this misery.

Fifteen feet below the long rolling swells on the surface, the Tiger shark swam along at a steady pace. She was a big female, thirteen feet in length and weighing almost eleven hundred pounds. The shark was on a journey, heading due east, out to the deep canyons along the eastern coast one hundred miles away. Although she was not capable of knowing or caring why, instinct plotted her course. The shark first sensed, then felt, and finally, saw the object drifting with the currents on the surface.

The ocean was transparent for fifteen feet below the surface. Lolita saw the gray, striped animal streaking up from the depths, but nothing registered in her mind. She lay on her side on the raft with her head resting on a small duffel bag. The soothing sound and gentle feeling of the lapping waves washing across the deck had lulled her into a semi-conscious state. Even when she saw the shark's white underbelly and huge rows of teeth as its mouth opened, she did not respond to what her half-open eyes saw. Only when the old man vanished, seemingly sucked off the raft, did Lolita's eyes snap fully open as she sprang upright to a sitting position.

The old man didn't feel the shark bite him. He had been lying on his back with his arms at his sides and his legs hanging over the edge, under water from the knee down. He only became aware of a powerful vise like object clamping down on his leg and pulling him off the raft. As the old man's head went under water, he realized that by some miracle he was free from whatever had grabbed him. The large shark's tail brushed his face as it swam away from him. Panic swept over Dannillo Hetes as he began to understand what had just taken place. Eyes wide, he stroked for the surface and the raft, now six feet away.

Lolita was on her knees, with the duffel bag she had used as a pillow opened and in front of her. She saw her grandfather's head break the surface. The twelve-year-old wanted to help as her grandfather tried to pull himself on board the raft, but she could not take her eyes from the huge, terrifying dorsal fin that was making a slow, wide circle back to the raft. Just as Dannillo pulled the upper half of his emaciated body onto the raft, the shark put on an incredible burst of speed. The old man almost had his hips and legs swung back upon the raft, when the big Tiger struck.

With her front end coming out of the water, the shark closed its jaws around the old man's midsection. The speed

3

and momentum of the shark driving into Dannillo knocked the wind from him and drove both man and shark towards the center of the raft. The weight of the shark forced the raft to sink a foot under the waves. Lolita was quick to act. Although she was frightened beyond belief, her only thought was to make the shark stop.

With her right hand, she reached into the duffel bag and lifted out a well-worn single action revolver. The gun was sixty years old and had belonged to her father before his death. Holding the heavy gun with her two small hands, Lolita pulled the hammer back, pointed it in the direction of the shark and pulled the trigger. At the sound of the shot, the shark released its death grip and slid back into the blue water. With a sweep of her tail, the Tiger shark dove toward the depths and was gone; giving no sign of whether Lolita's shot had found its mark.

Captain Lynn Meyers stood behind the wheel of her thirty-five-foot sport fishing boat. She held a pair of binoculars up to her pale green eyes and was concentrating on what she could see so much, that she jumped when Charlie entered the bridge.

"Cap'n, we're drifting away from the fish. We need to come about to be over 'em again," he said in a polite voice.

"Charlie, there's something out there." Lynn handed him the binoculars. "There," she said, pointing. "East by North-East."

Charlie Jones was sixty years old. He had started working on fishing boats at the age of eleven. For the last twenty of those years, Charlie had worked for Lynn's father Ross. When Ross passed away six years ago, and left his boat and charter fishing service to Lynn, Charlie stayed on as mate. He was an old salt, who looked and acted the part. He had known Lynn since she was a little girl, and now as a thirty-six-year-old captain, he trusted her with his life. That was why he continued to look through the binoculars, searching the royal blue swells, even though he could not see anything.

Lynn spoke in a calm tone, "You have to wait until the swells lift both us and whatever is out there, at the same time."

After a few seconds, Charlie saw a small dark object rise on a four-foot wave two miles away and then drop out of sight as the wave passed beneath. "Yup, I see it."

"Can you tell what it is?" Lynn asked.

"No ... too far. It's not very big. Could be debris ... could be a lot of things."

"Let's go see," Lynn said. "You take the helm and I'll secure the rods and inform the passengers."

Charlie looked doubtful. He raised his eyebrows and said, "Mr. Arbogast won't like this."

As she turned and exited the bridge, Lynn replied with confidence, "You take us over there, I'll handle Mr. Arbogast." She wore white, loose fitting cotton pants and a long-sleeved safari shirt. The short ponytail of her auburn hair protruded through the opening in the back of a long-billed cap. The outfit gave her fair, freckled skin protection from the sun. At five foot four, one hundred and eighteen pounds, the two men and their wives who were her passengers for the day each outsized Lynn. However, fishing was Lynn's life and the rules of the sea were like gospel to her.

Her determination and strong will prevented anyone from pushing her around.

She was the Captain and that was that.

Striding out onto the fishing deck, she spoke to the four people who made up the party, "It looks like the fish have moved on. I am going to secure the rods and gear until we find them again. Meanwhile, there is something adrift a few miles to our east. We're going to take a run over and see what it is." Fred Arbogast, who had arranged and paid for Lynn's charter services, spoke up, "Now wait a minute, I am paying you so we can catch ... "

Speaking in a firm voice, Lynn cut him off. "Something is out there Mr. Arbogast. We are going to see what it is." Without giving him a chance to reply, she smiled and added. "Don't worry; we'll be hauling Spanish mackerel over the side again before you know it."

When Charlie eased the boat to a stop, everyone crowded the port rail. All four passengers, along with Captain Meyers, had a look of astonishment on their faces as they gawked at the scene below them. On top of a beleaguered, half-submerged raft, a small girl knelt over an old man's bloodied body. The girl's bedraggled, dark hair hung loosely around her shoulders. Tattered clothing clung to her gaunt frame.

Lynn heard the girl softly sobbing. "Hey there!" she called. When she didn't get a reply, she tried again in Spanish, "Hola!"

This got the girl's attention. Her head spun around and she stared through big, brown, teary eyes at Lynn and the people on her boat.

"Hold on," Lynn continued in Spanish. "I am coming down to help you."

While Charlie kept the idling boat alongside the raft, Lynn went to a storage compartment built into the side of her craft. She opened it and took out a fifty-foot length of light, half-inch rope. Lynn tied one end of the rope around her waist. She used a bowline knot to secure the other end to the rail. Looking at Fred Arbogast she said, "Will you keep an eye on the raft? It doesn't look very seaworthy. With my extra weight, it may sink."

A look of disgust came over Arbogast's face. "You have got to be kidding! These people are probably illegal immigrants. This is none of our business."

"They are in trouble," Lynn insisted.

"So, call the Coast Guard, or something."

Lynn stood her ground. "Now you listen to me," she said, scolding, staring Arbogast straight in the eye. "I am the Captain of this vessel and I am going to help these poor souls. The rules of the sea state that a Captain should always help someone in distress on the open ocean. It's not like they have any other choices, if we don't help them they may die." She hesitated. "Think about it, what if that was you or your wife or daughter out there?"

7

Fred Arbogast was an influential executive who was used to being in control. His face flushed with anger at the thought of someone making him look like an inhuman jerk, especially in front of his partner and both of their wives.

Resentment filled his eyes as he leaned against the rail grabbing a loop of the rope that dangled over the side, but he said nothing.

When Lynn slid over the side and dropped effortlessly onto the raft, the little girl started

speaking in a dry, cracked voice. Lynn knelt beside her and they had a short conversation in

Spanish. When they finished talking, Lynn reached down and carefully took the girl in her arms. The stale smell of salt and sweat permeated the girl's straggly hair. She felt how light the emaciated girl was as she lifted her up to one of the men on the boat. Speaking to Arbogast's wife, Lynn said, "This is Lolita. Get her some water." Arbogast's partner reached under Lolita's arms and hoisted her aboard, while Mrs. Arbogast went to a cooler to fetch a bottle of water. Fred Arbogast said nothing but continued to hold on to the rope that was keeping Lynn out of the sea.

Lynn knelt once more on the rolling deck of the raft, beside the old man. She saw the man was in rough shape. His right leg was gone below the knee. A large duffel bag hung from his left leg. Lynn imagined this was to keep him from falling off the raft. Blood seeped from the crude bandage that Lolita had fashioned from a spare T-shirt and applied to the stump.

Several large wounds in his abdomen, which Lynn knew were bite marks, were oozing dark blood. The old man was trying to speak, but in his weakened condition, Lynn could only make out a word here and there. It sounded to Lynn like he said "Take..." and a word she could not understand, then "treasure..." and another word she could not understand. He ended with "Lolita ... future."

These were the last words ever spoken by Dannillo Hetes.

With a last gasp, the old man grabbed Lynn by the arm and pushed a packet into her hand.

He let out a sigh and passed away.

Before she could stop it from happening, a wave tipped the raft and the man slid off and into the sea. She reached for a hold on his arm, but he slipped into the deep. Lynn barely kept herself from falling off the edge. As she watched helplessly, the old man's body sank beneath the surface dragged down by the heavy duffel bag, which contained shoes and the gun. Soon it was out of sight, lost to the sea. Lynn looked at the object in her hand. She was holding a plastic, watertight storage bag. The contents of the bag astounded her. Through the clear material, she stared at what seemed to be an old map.

Chapter Two

A dense, damp mist shrouded Kill Devil Hills, North Carolina. Cool morning air mixed with the warm ocean water to create a rolling fog across the Outer Banks. Through blue eyes, Art Kendall gazed at the ocean. From where he stood in the bedroom of his weekend home, Art could see for many miles on an ordinary morning. Visibility was limited to twenty yards off shore on this morning.

The home was small with just three rooms. There was a combined kitchen and living room, a bathroom and the bedroom. Most of the wall of the bedroom facing the ocean was a wide, panoramic expanse of glass. Built on stilts, the home was no more than one-hundred feet from the water line at high tide.

Barb Kendall stirred in the bed. Rolling from her back to her side, she opened one eye and stared at her husband. From behind Barb did not think Art looked forty. She was thirty-five and Art could be mistaken for someone younger than her. The lines at his eyes and craggy features of his face were all that gave his age away. Watching him stand in front of the window, Barb absorbed every inch of his five-foot nine, one-hundred and eighty-pound body. Art had a deep tan, almost as dark as her own. She knew his body well, but never tired of seeing it. She could see it then in detail, for Art wore just two items, a Timex Expedition watch and a pair of boxer shorts.

Opening her other eye, Barb's gaze traveled from his strong legs, across his well-sculpted back, and up to his blonde head. The flattop haircut fit him well. Trim, straightforward, no nonsense; that described Art perfectly.

Art pulled on a pair of running shorts and a sleeveless sweatshirt. He did not notice that his wife was awake until he heard her speak.

"Hey baby, you going for a run?"

"Yes ma'am. I'm sorry I woke you."

"That's OK," Barb replied, yawning. "What time is it any way?"

"Five thirty-three."

Patting the bed beside her, Barb said in an alluring manner, "I can think of better things to do at five thirty-three in the morning."

Art feigned innocence, "But honey, I'm not tired."

Barb's lips parted in a sexy smile. "Oh, you're not going to sleep."

Art gazed at his wife, stretched out on the bed. He knew nothing covered her except the sheets. At five-foot six, Barb did not have the build of a runway model. Her body was filled out, athletic, but not stocky.

Her shoulder length dark brown hair was tussled and

she probably had stale breath now. Nevertheless, when Art looked at those warm brown eyes, he wanted nothing more than to be with her.

A disturbance came from outside that captured Art's attention. He heard voices coming from the beach below, men's voices. Turning to the window, Art saw two men and a dog on the beige sandy beach below. Both men, who were each getting on in years, stood face to face. They were involved in a heated argument.

The dog, it seemed, did not have a care in the world.

Art watched the yellow Labrador Retriever frolicking at the edge of surf. Tail wagging, the dog bounced from one interesting thing to the next.

"Goddamned idiots," Art said. He made an irritated growl.

Patting the bed once more, Barb pleaded, "The noise won't bother me, Come back to bed."

"No, it wouldn't bother me either, but I'd better straighten this out before someone gets hurt."

"Who's going to get hurt? Those guys are about a hundred years old."

Art laughed and replied, "I've seen this before, and both of those men have egos the size of Canada. Neither one will back down until someone talks some sense into them."

"Be careful," Barb joked.

Art caught the quip and smiled, saying, "I may as well go for my run while I'm down there."

Barb closed her eyes and sighed. "You know where to find me. Wake me when you finish your good deed for the day, Boy Scout."

"When I get back, you'll find out exactly what's on this Boy Scout's mind."

After Art left, Barb tried to sleep, but it was no use. She was wide awake now. Her thoughts were of her husband. She had called him a Boy Scout, but he was more of a man than anyone she had ever known. He was strong, honest and caring. Art was a rugged individualist, the rarest kind of man who made his own way through life. Barb could not imagine life without him.

At last, she climbed out of bed. She threw on an oversized t-shirt of Art's and went to the window. Peering down, Barb saw her husband speaking with the older men. Though she could not quite hear exactly what they were saying, she could make out the aggravated tones of her neighbors. She also heard Art's calm, steady voice. Gradually, the pitch of the men's voices declined. Soon, all three men were speaking in peaceful voices.

"You are a Boy Scout Art, and you're my hero," Barb whispered aloud.

Once Art had finished his four-mile run along the beach, the fog began to clear. Entering the house, he found Barb dressed in cutoff shorts and a swimsuit top. She stood by the counter slicing a Cantaloupe. Surprised at seeing her out of bed, Art asked, "What are you doing up?"

"How can I sleep while my Knight in shining armor is out slaying Dragons?"

"Oh hell, they're not Dragons, just lonely old men. You were right. They are harmless. The two of them enjoy arguing. I think it gives them something to do."

"Let me guess, Gene's dog is crapping all over Ted's property?"

"Yea, something like that. The funny thing is, if anything ever happened to that dog, I don't know who would be more upset, Gene or Ted."

"Or Art," Barb added.

"I don't care about that mangy mongrel," Art said, taking off his sweatshirt.

Barb smiled. After ten years of marriage, Art's answer did not fool her. Cleo was a big-hearted dog and everyone in the small coastal community of Kill Devil Hills loved her; even the big-hearted dog she had married. Carrying a plate of fruit, she walked over to Art and asked, "What do you want to do first, eat breakfast or take a shower?"

"This Boy Scout thought he might try to earn a merit badge."

Barb stepped closer and whispered. "How would you do that?"

"I thought maybe I could help a certain lady across the street."

As the cherry-red sphere of the sun nestled into the west behind her, Barb's vacant stare fell upon the sea. With her feet propped on the railing of the beach house porch, she leaned back in the soft cushioned deck chair. She loved being close to the ocean in the evening. The setting sun provided a soft, mellow light, which lent a sinuous beauty to the surroundings.

Closing the book, she had been reading, *Homecoming*, Barb inhaled a long breath. The light was becoming too low for reading. This was the time that she often found pleasure in being alone, a time where she could think, reflect on the past and wonder about the future.

Art had gone up to Kitty Hawk surfing with two of the neighborhood boys and would not be back for a while.

She let her thoughts meander and tonight those thoughts were of the past. Barb allowed her memory to carry her back to her youth. Born and raised in a small suburb outside of Denver, she had grown up with the outgoing personality of someone living a healthy life in the outdoors.

Her parents enjoyed camping in the alpine meadows and Barb developed a passion for exploring at an early age. Hiking, snowboarding, and fly-fishing held her attention throughout her youth.

She had never played sports in school, but because she grew up and lived as a tomboy her entire life, Barb knew Adventure Racing was for her the moment she first heard of it. Combining physical skills with mental toughness in the most remote outdoor theatres played right to Barb's strengths. She excelled at orienteering and team social dynamics. She also kept herself in tiptop condition. A love of the outdoors added to her resumé.

When she started Adventure Racing just out of the University of Colorado, Barb found herself drawn to the outdoorsy men of her sport. Leaders of teams who got to the finish line no matter the obstacle became her male companions until she met Art.

During the first weeks of their relationship, Barb felt like a scientist who discovered a new species. She had been involved in several intimate and social relationships with men, but Art Kendall was a completely different animal. Excited, amazed and awed by his presence, she had known from the beginning that they were a match. Barb would never forget the first words he spoke to her.

She had been selected by the team leader to join the racing team sponsored by Kendall Outdoors Adventure and Supply Company. Word was that the man behind the company was a one of a kind, self-made man who had started from scratch and now owned and operated a worldwide business. Though she had never met the man in person, on occasion, Barb would overhear bits and pieces of his exploits. She brushed this idle talk off as nothing more than rumors and gossip.

The truth of the story was that Art Kendall *had* started Kendall Outdoor and Adventure from scratch. After Art finished his service in the United States Marine Corps, he worked as a river guide. With his physical abilities, love of the outdoors, and outgoing personality, he excelled at his profession. In a few short years, he started his own company. Kendall Outdoors and Adventure, now called Kendall Outdoors, offered guided rafting, trekking and survival courses.

The rivers and mountains of Art's home state of North Carolina provided the destinations for the adventures for the first few years. Soon however, Kendall Outdoors was offering trips across North and South America. Mountain climbing was added to the list of adventures.

The best guides in the business worked for the company. Art used only the best equipment. Word spread fast through the adventure enthusiast community. Kendall Outdoors soon became known as a top-notch name in the industry.

The logistics of moving and setting up equipment and camps in remote locations required an extensive network. A big reason for his success was his ability to recruit good quality people. Art Kendall had a presence. People were eager to work with and assist him. Hollis James and a few others became his go-to connections. They were the people who got things done. Acting as private contractors, they set-up, moved, arranged or did whatever was needed to get the job done. They were Art's contacts who had their own contacts. Art orchestrated everything and provided first class service to his clients.

Exotic, once in a lifetime locations were scouted for the trip, oftentimes by Art himself. At first, he had some T-shirts and caps made up just for the staff. Next, he began to offer these items for sale to customers. The Kendall logo carried a great deal of clout, and soon came to be in high demand. Soon, Kendall Outdoor launched an entire brand name line.

The sport of Adventure Racing proved to be a perfect mesh for Art's business. His company started sponsoring teams. Next, Kendall Outdoors sponsored races and eventually Art organized his own events.

As the sport gained popularity, some of the races got television coverage. When Art could not settle a dispute over production rates, he invested in a small production company of his own. He brought the company into the Kendall fold where it blossomed into a multi-million-dollar enterprise. Eventually, the production company even grew into its own channel broadcasting all types of outdoor activities and sports along with full-length adventure films and docudramas.

More than once, white collar, business insiders lamented on Art Kendall's ability to make a success of everything he touched. Offers poured in inviting Art to step out into other business ventures. Art made the decision to keep his hand close to his chest. Other than a few small outside investments, his Adventure Company remained his focus in life. With headquarters in Ashville, North Carolina and another office in Los Angeles, Kendall Outdoors thrived.

Chapter Three

The race took place in the Patagonia region of Argentina. Barb's team had been traversing a high jagged mountain peak, when an unexpected, violent storm blew in. The wind picked up and the temperature dropped. Freezing rain and driving snow pelted the racers. Barb slipped on loose ground and broke her ankle and leg in two places. At the time, her team was six to seven hours ahead of the second-placed team.

The rules of the race declared that to win or even qualify as finishing the race, all four team members had to cross the finish line. With Barb out of action, her team faced disqualification. At first, she was disgusted for having cost her team and their sponsor the race. As the night wore on however, it became apparent that she might not make it off the mountain alive. The conditions made a helicopter landing impossible. Barb was losing blood and body heat as the stinging snow and howling wind blew across the mountain.

At around ten o'clock that night, she heard Josh Sampson talking on his two-way radio. When he finished,

Josh padded through the snow to where Bucky Knolls sat beside where she lay.

"You're not gonna believe this," Josh said to Bucky, his voice filled with wonderment. Kneeling in the snow beside Barb, he placed a hand on her shoulder, "Hang in there, Barb. Art Kendall is on his way. He's leading a team of volunteers up the mountain to take you off. They'll be here in a few hours."

As the hours passed, Barb could not help but wonder who this man was. What kind of man, a millionaire no less, would risk his life climbing a monstrous mountain in the dead of night, during a full-blown blizzard, to help someone he did not even know? An even more pertinent question was, how did he persuade anyone else to follow his lead?

Barb eventually passed out. When she came to, she saw a pair of bright blue eyes staring back at her. They were the most alive, vibrant, smiling eyes she had ever seen. Art Kendall was kneeling on one knee, with his warm hand on her forehead. He must have just arrived Barb thought, because she could see ice hanging from his eyebrows and snow plastered to his cheeks. The strain of hiking all night in adverse weather conditions was etched in the lines of his face. Then, he smiled and in a gentle voice, spoke those famous first words, "Goddamned nice weather we're having, isn't it?"

Barb managed a small smile and stammered, "I ... well yea ... I guess." This was the first time in her life she ever remembered becoming tongue-tied.

"These men are Doctors Walsh and McNally. They are

going to take care of you so we can get you home." Without waiting for a reply, Art nodded to the doctors, rose and trod over to Josh, who was standing fifteen feet away.

The doctors busied themselves with their chore. They inserted an I.V. line into Barb's veins and went to work bandaging and splinting her fractured bones. Barb's thoughts were on Art Kendall however, and her eyes followed him to where he stood beside Jim.

"Damn good to see you Jim."

"Good to see you Art," Jim replied, with earnest appreciation. "Do you think we can get her down?"

Art stood as straight as a concrete pillar against the wind and driving snow. He looked Jim straight in the eye, "You bet your ass we're going to get her down. Now here's what we're going to do ... "

Barb closed her eyes and heard the voice trail away as the wind carried it down the slope. She felt safe for the first time in hours. A sense of contentment enveloped her. She knew that if Art Kendall were around, somehow things would be all right. Either that or the morphine had started to kick in.

Educated and with a strong sense of self, Barb knew the intricacies of hero-victim relationships. When Art insisted on going along with her in the ambulance, she thought he was being brotherly, nothing more. Later, when he started to make regular visits to the hospital, Barb didn't allow herself to be swept away by her emotions. While recovering in the days and weeks following the accident however, she became even more impressed with Art.

The way he handled the hordes of reporters asking for interviews proved to be nothing short of a class act. When a reporter asked a question, Art usually deferred to another member of the rescue crew saying something along the lines of, "Doc Walsh really saved the day up there. He's the one you should be talking to." He would pull the doctor to the front of the cameras and melt away into the crowd. When a reporter did pin him down alone, Art answered all questions with courtesy, always downplaying his own role and building up the other men.

Barb watched these interviews on television from her hospital room. When Art visited, she always waited for him to mention the fact that he had been on TV but he never did.

Another thing that Barb admired was the fact that Art's outdoor business did not profit from her accident. There was no ad campaign featuring the gear used to rescue a woman from sure death on a mountain in Argentina. No commercialization, nothing.

Not so, for the other people who were on the mountain that night. The three other members of the team and all seven members of the rescue crew became instant celebrities. For two nineteen-year-old local boys who went along on the rescue, the trip up the mountain became a career move. They became very successful wilderness guides with a high paying international clientele. Before that night, the two had been nothing more than strong winded, dirt poor, backwoods boys. Both doctors ran the talk show circuit sharing the story with millions of TV viewers. Another of

the volunteer rescuers even wrote a best-selling book titled
RACE THE MOUNTAIN.

Art wanted no part of it. He was not shy or introverted,
just not interested. On one occasion, soon after Barb's release from the hospital, she asked Art why he was so modest. His reply was "Modest? Hell, I'm not modest; it's in the
past, over and done."

Barb now knew it was one of the traits that made her
husband tick. While some people spend most of their lives
looking back, he was always focused one hundred percent
on the present or looking to the future.

Barb could not help herself. Little by little, she fell for
this man until she knew he was the only man for her. She
did not fall for one act of courage on a mountaintop, but for
the whole man. Her memory picked up speed as she breezed
through the past eight years. She felt as if she was an in-
jured athlete one day and married to the man of her dreams
the next.

The afternoon sun had burned off the fog. As the sun set in
the west, North Carolina's Outer Banks were cast in a soft
hue. This perfect light was what they were waiting for. A
young man and woman paddled kayaks through the surf
and up onto the sandy beach where another young man and
woman waited. Both the men and women had strong, athletic builds. When the couple climbed out of their boats,
they flashed brilliant white teeth as they smiled and con-

versed with the other couple on the beach. They gestured with their arms, nodded their heads and spoke about absolutely nothing.

From a folding beach chair, a frumpy man yelled, "Cut! That's good, but we can do better. I want to see more adrenaline. Paddle harder. Don't crawl out of the boats, jump out." The overweight director cleared his throat and addressed the couple standing on the beach, "When you guys go to greet them, don't saunter, run! This commercial is about health and vigor. Our customers want to see action. All right people, let's try it again."

From where he stood, ten feet behind the director, Art stifled a chuckle. Although the company shooting the commercial was a division of Kendall Outdoors, he did not usually attend the shoots. Normally, he would only see the final product so he could approve or disapprove. However, with the director shooting the commercial practically in Art's back yard, he thought it would be fun to watch the process.

Assistants rushed up to the actors fussing with the Kendall Outdoor apparel the actors wore. Someone groomed hair. One person brushed sand from the actors' legs. After the man and woman paddled their kayaks back out through the surf, an assistant brushed the footprints from the sand making it look like no one had recently stepped there.

Art turned from the action and walked over to where Barb rested in a lounge chair with her bare feet in the sand. She turned off a mini tablet as Art approached, giving him her full attention.

"How's the shoot going?" she asked.

"It's a hell of a racket, I'll say that."

"You mean you don't want to give up your business life to become a famous Hollywood producer?"

"Christ, no."

"You never know, you might like it. You'd have all those little Hollywood actresses fawning over you."

Art laughed. "No, it's not for me."

"You could get divorced six or seven times. Have your picture in all the tabloid papers. Go on the talk show circuit ... wear your sunglasses inside one of your many houses. Fame, isn't it what everyone wants?"

"OK," Art said. "You talked me into it, but only if you're my agent."

Barb smiled and said, "Anytime Art. Anytime."

"The first thing I'd do is get rid of about half of that crew."

"You couldn't do that."

"Sure, I could."

"An actor can't fire the crew Art."

"If he has the right agent he can," Art quipped.

Barb laughed. "What's wrong with the crew?" she asked.

"There's nothing wrong with them. They just get on my nerves, fussing with every little thing. I could've had this thing done in about half the time," Art explained as he sat down next to her.

"That's their job and it's why the finished product turns

out so good."

Art said, "Yes I know. Joking aside, they do a hell of a good job. It's not for me though."

"Oh well, I guess I'll have to put up with being married to a man who's not a famous Hollywood actor." Barb pouted.

Art smiled and winked at her. It had been a busy day and he had not seen much of his wife since early morning. "So how was your day, anything new?"

"No, nothing really. You did get an e-mail from the captain of the boat you have chartered. He says he's on to some good fish and looking forward to your arrival next week."

The charter Barb spoke of was Art's involvement in the White Marlin Open off the coast of Maryland. Art was an avid saltwater angler and he loved competing in Billfish Tournaments around the world.

"That sounds great. Are we packed for the trip?"

"Pretty much. There are still a few things to do."

"Outstanding. I'll call the office in the morning while we're en route." With a glint in his eye, Art said, "I plan on winning this tournament."

Barb smiled and nodded. She knew he had a good chance. When her husband set his mind to do something, he was hard to stop.

Chapter Four

Something was wrong. In the thirty years, she had known him; Lynn had never known Charlie to be late. Any other morning, he would be here at the dock, readying the boat for tomorrow's charter. Lynn used her smart phone to call once more. Charlie was old school. He did not own a cell phone, but still relied on a traditional house phone. After eleven rings, she hung up. Something was wrong. She could almost feel it.

Lynn Meyers began to relive the events of the previous day. After making sure the young girl was in no immediate danger, Lynn headed straight for her homeport on the key of Islamorda. She dropped Charlie and the paying customers off at the dock. Lolita remained on board the boat while Lynn had refueled. Running the boat hard, they had reached Miami late last night. Lynn paid for an overnight slip at the harbor. She moored the boat and took a cab straight to the address of Lolita's relatives.

That was when things got strange. Lolita's aunt and uncle were very happy to see her. They were also saddened to hear of the old man's death. However, when Lynn showed them the packet containing the map, they acted as if she had the plague. Lolita's relatives wanted nothing to do with Lynn or the map. She was shown to the door and shooed away.

Riding through the dark streets of Miami in the back seat of a cab, Lynn had gotten a strange feeling. She began to put the pieces together. There could be but one reason for Lolita's relatives to act the way they did. Someone was after the map. Somehow, the Aunt and Uncle knew some-one was after the map.

Paying her fare, Lynn got out of the cab and strode at a brisk clip along the shadowy dock to her slip. She had the feeling someone was watching her. The fine hair on the back of her neck stood up. Glancing over her shoulder Lynn expected to find someone stalking her, but she saw no one. Once she reached her boat, her nerves were tattered. Wasting little time, Lynn untied the moorings, started the engine and headed out to sea. During the overnight trip, back to Islamorda, Lynn settled down. The Captain had let her imagination get the best of her. She needed to be rational. She needed some sleep.

Now, something *was* wrong. Charlie was never late. The feeling she had the previous night had returned. Lynn was dead tired. She wanted nothing more than to fill Charlie in on events since she dropped him off. She would leave Charlie to take care of the boat, while she went home to catch up on her rest. Lynn was looking forward to a long, hot shower and eight hours of sleep.

Throwing the packet on the passenger seat of her Ford Explorer, Lynn slipped the car into drive and drove away from the dock. Charlie's house was five miles away. Lynn covered the distance in less than ten minutes. Rolling down Charlie's crushed seashell driveway, Lynn noticed his 1990 Dodge truck parked beside his shed. She halted by his front door, got out and knocked. When no reply came, Lynn knocked again and called, "Charlie, are you here? Charlie!"

Disgruntled seagulls arguing over a piece of food were the only sounds she heard. Lynn decided to look around. Thinking she might find him in the shed, Lynn crossed the small yard. As she passed Charlie's rusty old pick-up truck, Lynn noticed the keys were in the ignition. That wasn't right. The swinging doors of the shed were ajar. The hairs on her neck prickled again and Lynn stepped up carefully, sidling along until she could stare through the gap between the doors.

Her eyes widened. Lynn became shaky and felt dizzy. She thought the scene before her would kill her. The next thing Lynn knew, she was lying on the ground. Sharp edges of the shells Charlie used for paving, cut her hands and knees. Lynn was unsure of herself. Where am I? What's going on? At last, she said aloud, "Charlie."

Lynn scrambled to her feet and looked inside the shed once more. The grizzly scene had not changed. Lynn saw her mate Charlie, hanging ten feet off the ground from a rope. The rope was around his neck and tied to the rafters. She knew from his glazed over eyes, he was dead.

Walter Ulrich took a swallow from his bottle of beer and gazed through brown eyes at his surroundings. Skipper's, an open-air bar on Key West, was just beginning to fill with the evening crowd. It was nine o'clock and many of the locals were heading home for the night, replaced by many more tourists.

Walt wore Teva sandals and olive green cargo shorts. A green print, original Aloha shirt covered his six-foot, one-hundred-and-seventy-pound frame. He was very fit for a thirty-seven-year-old man, with a deep chest, broad shoulders and a narrow waist. His dark brown hair showed no signs of gray or balding. "This is definitely the life," he said, as he leaned back in his chair, shielded his eyes from the lowering sun and let out a contented sigh.

Brock McGowen, who sat across the small table from Walt agreed, "You got that right brother." Brock was dressed similarly to Walt. The only difference was the colors. The men were the same age, but Brock had a shorter and thicker build. Standing five-foot-eight, and weighing two hundred pounds, Brock was not quick moving, but he was quick thinking. He was also as strong as an ox. Brock carried most of his weight in bulky muscle, with just the beginning of a spare tire around his mid-section. The gray sprouting up in his coal black hair and thick mustache made Brock appear considerably older than Walt.

Brock took a long swig of his beer and stared at the bottle. "How do they make it so good, so cheap?" he wondered aloud.

Brock loved beer. He loved to talk about beer. He was an intelligent, well-traveled man, who knew the risks of over indulgence. Even so, being born and raised in Minnesota, Brock talked about such things as beer, cheese, the Vikings, and Polish sausage with a passion. Nodding in the direction of the DJ, who was setting up for the evening, he asked, "I wander if that guy plays polkas?"

"Polkas?" Walt asked.

"Sure," Brock answered, looking around the dimly lit bar, "I'll bet a few of these lovely young ladies have been waiting their entire lives for a handsome Midwesterner to come along and teach them how to polka."

Walt simply shook his head and laughed.

The third member of their group, Denny Smith, arrived at the table, pulled out a chair and sat down. Denny was two years younger than Walt and Brock. He was six-foot two inches tall, lanky, with sandy hair, and gray eyes. While Brock came across as a joker, Denny projected quiet intelligence. On his way, back from the men's room, Denny overheard Brock's comments and decided to have some fun. In a voice that sounded deadly serious, he remarked, "I've been thinking, maybe we shouldn't take any beer along on the trip."

Brock raised an eyebrow and said, "That's crazy talk."

Walt caught on and played along, "Good idea Denny, it'll give us more room on the boat to bring back the gold."

"Yea, and by the way," Denny kept on, "I overheard a couple of good looking women over by the rest room say they wished some goofy Midwesterner would teach them to polka."

Walt and Denny burst out laughing. Knowing he was the recipient of their joke, Brock joined in the laughter.

Walt and Brock worked as Federal Mine Inspectors. They worked together often and had been friends for ten years. Denny was a construction superintendent. He met Walt and Brock on a job site five years ago, and the three men became quick friends. The trip Denny spoke of earlier was their annual treasure hunt. Each year the men took a three-week vacation from their jobs and traveled to the Florida Keys to search for long lost shipwrecks. They did rent gear and search for treasure, but the trip was recreational above all else. The men also snorkeled, drank a little beer, went sea kayaking, and did a good deal of just plain relaxing.

This would be the third trip the men had taken together. So far, they had not found anything of worth on the previous two. This would be the one they struck it rich on was the running joke every year. Not one of the three men believed they would ever find anything, but they were the adventurous type. Searching for sunken treasure was more exciting than laying on a beach somewhere.

"Well," Brock said, rising from his seat at the table, "we'll see who has the last laugh." His friends watched as Brock strode over to an attractive woman at the bar and started a conversation. Before long, the woman was laughing and seemed to be enjoying Brock's company.

"You have to admit," Denny said, "as goofy as he is, he

sure does meet his share of women."

"He sure does," agreed Walt, smiling. Taking another swallow of beer, he said, "That's it for me. I'm going to take a short walk before heading to the boat."

"Yes, this is my last one too, five o'clock comes early. I'll see you back on the boat."

Skipper's was located only fifty yards from the docks. Walt stepped outside and felt a cool breeze drifting in off the ocean. Dark clouds had begun to form over the Keys and flashes of lightning periodically lit up the western sky. From the sound of rolling thunder in the distance, Walt estimated that he had at least a half an hour before the storm reached shore. The weather forecast called for thunderstorms through the night and into the morning, followed by bright sunshine and calm seas the next few days. Better to have a storm tonight, rather than after we've gone out to sea, Walt thought as he walked along Duvall Street and down the narrow wooden path leading to Key West Bight Marina.

Inhaling deeply, Walt relished the scent and taste of the fresh, salty air. He always found it difficult, almost impossible to describe the ocean to someone who had never seen it. The sound of the waves breaking on the beach. Feeling the foam and salt stinging the eyes and leaving a taste on the lips and, of course, the air. He felt sorry for anyone who hadn't known those things

Coastal living was something Walt missed from his childhood. His parents owned and operated a small motel in Pleasantville New Jersey, a suburb of Atlantic City. Growing up, Walt lived only twenty minutes from the ocean. Family trips to the beach were a regular occurrence. As soon as Walt could drive, he would borrow his parents' car, drive to the Beach, and spend whole summer days swimming in the surf of Atlantic City's beaches.

The motel also had a large pool. Walt loved the water and took to it naturally. By age fifteen, he was the fastest swimmer in a county of fast swimmers. Walt continued to excel at swimming throughout high school, earning a scholarship to Rutgers University. He was the top swimmer on his college team, setting many school records. He spent summers working as a lifeguard for the Atlantic City beach patrol.

Walt also enjoyed the wilderness; hiking, camping, white water kayaking. While on a hiking trip in the Pocono Mountains of Pennsylvania, Walt suffered a fractured leg. He was in his senior year at Rutgers at the time, and headed for the U.S. Olympic team. The injury healed completely in two months, but that was long enough to keep him off the team. Walt took it all in his stride, completing his studies and earning a degree.

As Walt strolled past the *Hunkered Down*, their boat for the trip, he gave it a quick once over. Built in 1979, the immaculately kept thirty-five foot Bruno sport fishing boat did not look or act her age. Four fuel tanks fed her powerful Caterpillar Diesel engine. Polished fixtures and fresh paint adorned her deck. Tempered, tinted windows provided a sleek look and privacy.

Not seeing anything unusual, Walt continued walking

and turned his attention to the fishing boat tied off to the dock beside the *Hunkered Down*. The boat floated in her slip with the bow toward the sea and the stern toward the dock. Walt could see the name painted in gold letters across the white stern, *Lit'l Lynny*.

Walt stopped walking when he noticed that the after deck of the boat looked like something was amiss. Ropes lay strewn about the deck, a small trashcan was overturned, and a tackle box was lying on its side. Most of the lures had spilled from the open box.

Walt found this strange; most of the captains he knew would never allow their boats to reach this level of disarray.

By late afternoon most of the supplies for the outing had already been loaded aboard the *Hunkered Down*. They stowed away their personal items, the groceries and most of the various dive gear needed for the trip. Brock and Denny worked at lashing down several large dry bags full of gear on the aft deck. The heavy-duty dry bags were watertight. Hollis James worked with Walt to secure the specialty dive gear required for the treasure hunt. A local inhabitant of the Florida Keys, Hollis was Walt's connection for the trip. Before the men departed for the open ocean, they always agreed to leave their smart phones with Hollis until they returned. All three of the men relished the short time away from their phones.

Hollis provided the boat and arranged for the delivery of most of the gear and necessities for the trip. At a glance, Hollis James appeared to be a bit slow. People have even called him backwards. From his too skinny build to his too slow speech and movements, he was sometimes mistaken for having a disability. To those who know Hollis, those impressions could not be more off target. Hollis James was a man who had found his niche. The people who worked with him gained an invaluable advantage. His exact job title was hard to pin point. In a nutshell, Hollis got things done.

He specialized in the in-between jobs. Anyone could ship cargo from point A to point B. However, if the cargo had to go by truck, then by boat, then plane, helicopter, and mule, Hollis was the go-to guy to get it there. If someone needed a floating helicopter pad built in the middle of the Pacific, he called Hollis. For transportation through Ecuador, or the Bronx for that matter, call Hollis. If your motorcycle broke down, Hollis could either fix it or find someone who could. He had contacts and resources all over the world. No one knew how he acquired such resources, but he did, and he got things done.

He never looked or dressed the part. He had a scraggly beard that would not fill in. He usually wore jeans, a T-shirt, an old ball cap, and sneakers. He drove an older model two-wheel drive pick-up truck. His modest house was built in 1975. The services Hollis provided demanded top dollar. Most years he earned two to three hundred thousand dollars. Hollis saved most of his income. His only indulgence was his fishing lure collection. Hollis liked to collect old fishing lures. While his collection would not bring millions of dollars at auction, he did have a vast array collected over the years. If Hollis James was not busy working at his business, you could bet he would be working on his collection.

Walt and Hollis were crouched down inspecting an air compressor on the dock when a booming voice with a distinctive Australian accent interrupted them. "Hello lads. Going to be doing a bit of salvaging, eh?"

They turned their attention to an enormous man standing in front of them on the dock. Walt sized the man up in an instant. He stood straight with his hands at his sides. Large white teeth showed through his grin. A thick, orange mustache covered his upper lip. The man had copper colored hair with a touch of grey showing at the temples worn close-cropped. He wore a large straw hat, which made him look even bigger. Walt did not find the man threatening but more, imposing. He stood about six-foot three and must have weighed two sixty. From the lines in his face, Walt guessed his age at early to mid-fifties.

Walt stood, stuck out his hand, and introduced himself, "Walter Ulrich."

The great bear of a man took Walt's hand in a firm handshake and said, "Billy Haggarty. How do you do."

"This is my friend Hollis," Walt said.

Hollis never pretended to be a people person. He merely nodded, not attempting to stand and shake Haggarty's hand.

Walt continued, "We're going to do a little recreational diving. How about you? What brings you here?"

"Business. Well actually, I do business in America. I keep a boat down here for recreation."

Walt was not a pushy person, but he did not believe in

beating around the bush. "What kind of business are you in?"

"Distribution mate. My home is in New Zealand, although I was born and raised in Australia, but I travel to wherever there is an opportunity."

"Sounds interesting."

"Not as interesting as searching for sunken treasure. They say there's still quite a good bit out there."

Walt smiled. "They say a lot of things, but a great deal of money has been spent searching ... more in fact, than all the treasure that has ever been recovered."

Haggarty stared out to sea. "That may be true, but don't forget the *Atocia.*"

Like every amateur treasure hunter around the Florida Straits, Walt was familiar with the story of the *Atocia.* Mel Fisher discovered the Spanish Galleon *Atocia* in 1985. Her cargo was worth hundreds of millions of dollars.

"Yes," Walt said, "but Mel Fisher spent 17 years searching for the *Atocia.*"

Haggarty pondered for a moment. Finally, he said, "Is that right?"

"It is. There were also millions of dollars spent before the bulk of the treasure was discovered."

The big Australian nodded and said, "Yes, I guess the vastness of the ocean combined with the effects of time would make treasure hunting a daunting task. I think I'll stick to distribution."

Walt laughed and said, "I won't be quitting my day job, that's for certain."

Haggarty wished Walt good luck and continued along the dock.

Chapter Five

Later that evening, just before dark, Walt took a last stroll along the docks. Hollis had returned home after he finished loading supplies aboard the boat. Brock and Denny were playing cards in the galley of the *Hunkered Down* after they had finished in the bar. Walt noticed dark clouds looming on the horizon. Some rain was normal for this time of year in the Keys. The warm air and water temperatures made for enjoyable time on the ocean regardless of the almost daily rain squalls.

As he neared the end of the dock, Walt heard a familiar voice.

"Walter! Come aboard old man." The voice belonged to Billy Haggarty, the big Australian they had met earlier that afternoon.

"Mr. Haggarty, hello," Walt replied. He climbed the gangway leading from the dock to Haggarty's yacht. The yacht was a beautiful fifty-eight-foot Sea Ray Lelass.

Haggarty shook Walt's hand and invited him to have a seat at a small table on the stern deck. The table rested under a canvas canopy. Plastic wire ties fastened an intercom to one of the posts supporting the canopy. When both men sat at the table, Haggarty pushed a button on the intercom and spoke, "Jonna, please bring two Sabbaths. We have a visitor."

Haggarty showed his huge smile while they waited in silence. In almost no time, a man appeared carrying a serving tray with two bottles of Pan Head Black Sabbath beer and two beer glasses. The man's skin was a dark tanned color. He had coal black, curly hair that hung down loosely to his shoulders. Tattoos covered his face.

In his heavy Australian accent, Haggarty said, "He's also my first mate."

"Nice to meet you," Walt said. He knew the Maori were the indigenous people of New Zealand. As they shook hands, he also found out that this one had a very strong grip.

Jonna nodded his head in greeting, then left Walt and Haggarty alone.

Walt found Billy Haggarty to be a friendly, outgoing man. He asked about and seemed genuinely interested in Walt's life. The men carried on an amiable conversation ranging from Haggarty's business to travel to global warming. Walt stayed aboard the Yacht for about twenty minutes, just the amount of time it took to finish the bottle of strong locally brewed New Zealand beer. Declining a second bottle, Walt bid Haggarty farewell and headed down the gangway to the dock.

A light drizzle began to fall as Walt strode along in the

direction of the *Hunkered Down*. Nearing the fishing vessel *Lit'l Lynny,* he noticed two men walking swiftly away. Walt stopped walking and slid a step to his right and into a shadow. Did the men come from the boat or were they just passing by? Walt did not know for sure but felt the need to stay out of sight.

He stood as still as a stone and watched in silence as the men walked away from him, fading into the darkness.

He thought it over for a few seconds.

The rain began to fall in earnest but Walt remained motionless.

Lightning lit up the night sky over the dock. Walt could not see anyone along the walkway now. Thunder rolled close to the waterfront. Finally, he started to walk again, slowly, cautiously, almost sneaking. Reaching the fishing boat, he found everything the same as it was when he had walked past earlier that evening. Another streak of lightning flashed directly overhead illuminating the entire dock area. Once again, he appeared to be alone. Walt shook his head and smiled. "My imagination must be running away with me; well, either my imagination or that strong New Zealand beer," he said aloud. Walt returned to the boat as the thunderstorm broiled over Key West.

***

The alarm on Walt's wristwatch sounded at five-thirty a.m. He turned the alarm off and wiped the sleep from his eyes. Sitting up and throwing his feet over the edge of the bunk, he heard steady rain. Sleep beckoned as he listened to the constant patter and felt the gentle rocking of the boat. Walt felt sorry for people who got seasick. To him, the most relaxing, therapeutic treatment in the world was to be on a boat on the ocean.

He pulled on a pair of shorts and a T-shirt. Opening the door separating the sleeping quarters from the galley, he found Denny pouring a cup of coffee.

"Morning," Denny said in a cheerful voice, handing the cup to Walt.

Walt took the cup and said, "You're up early."

Denny poured a second cup of coffee. "Doesn't it seem like it's always easier to get up in the morning when you're not getting up to go to work?"

"Yes, it does." Walt relished the taste of the coffee. "How is the construction business anyway?"

"Busy as ever. At least I'm as busy as ever. Even when things slow down, the company leaves it up to me to figure out how to do more with less. My job is one headache after another, long hours and not much time for flying."

Denny had learned to fly as a teenager. His father was an airline pilot who spent many hours teaching Denny and allowing him to experience the joy of flying. Denny did not care for the schedules airline pilots kept, but he loved to fly small planes whenever he had the chance. On any Sunday, he would be airborne in his Piper Sea Ray somewhere among the clouds.

Walt sat down at the small table in the center of the room. He unfolded a map of the area across the table. Studying the map, he traced his finger along a thin line. Drawn in pencil, the line ran from their current position to a spot marked with a circle. "How long do you think it will take, about four or five hours?" he asked.

"Visibility will be limited, and the sea a little rough. We'll take it slow. I estimate it'll take closer to six hours."

Their basic plan was the same every year. Through research before the trip, they would locate an area likely to hold a shipwreck. This never proved difficult. Hundreds of Spanish ships went down in the waters off Florida, Cuba and many of the Caribbean islands during the fifteenth and sixteenth centuries. Discovering one of these Centuries old wrecks was the difficult part.

Denny, being a pilot, was the best navigator. He would plot a course to get them to their destination. Once there, the more advanced divers Walt and Brock would go about scouring the sea floor in search of artifacts. Denny would make sure everything was all right top side. He would also handle most of the cooking and chores in the galley. Usually after five or six days of coming up empty handed, the men tired of treasure hunting. They focused on more enjoyable and relaxing activities for the rest of their trip.

Brock woke up just in time for breakfast, which consisted of eggs, bacon, toast, and home fries. Cleaning the last of the food from his plate, Brock remarked, "That was excellent Denny. A little heavy on the fat though, don't you think?"

Walt said, "If you can't indulge yourself on vacation, when can you?"

"Yea Brock, what's up with that?" Denny chimed in. "I slave over a hot stove all morning, and that's the thanks I get? We also have oat meal and cereal for tomorrow and you can prepare that yourself."

"Oat Meal, blah, I'd rather have a heart attack than eat that every day."

Walt laughed although he agreed with Brock's statement. At thirty-seven years of age, he was just beginning to have to watch what he ate. The jovial mood continued throughout breakfast. The beginning of a vacation, especially a treasure hunting adventure, always made for an expectant atmosphere.

Soon after breakfast, the men cast off and headed out to sea. Dawn had broken dark and gloomy, with steady rain falling. By nine a. m., they were two hours from the Marina on Key West. By this time, the rain had become intermittent, with periods of hard downpours and light drizzle. The *Hunkered Down* was thirty-five feet long from stem to stern. The large cabin above deck contained the wheelhouse and ample room for storage. Denny stood behind the wheel, staring out at the white caps as the boat plowed through a choppy, steel-gray sea. The swish, swish of the windshield wipers mesmerized Denny and he did not hear the door to the wheelhouse open.

Brock poked his head in and asked, "Is everything all right in here Denny?"

Startled, Denny tightened his grip on the wheel and froze. He relaxed at once however, and replied, "Everything's fine. Seems like the storm is breaking up."

"All right. Just checking," Brock said. "Give us a yell if you need anything." He closed the door and walked down the steps, into the galley. The galley was small, eight-feet by eight-feet. A door behind the stairs led to the engine room in the stern. Opposite this door was another that joined the sleeping quarters, which consisted of not much more than two bunk beds, to the galley. In between were a sink and cooking area. A pullout couch, a table and four chairs left little free space in the cramped galley.

Brock said, "I looked in on Denny. He's fine. I'm going out on to the rear deck for some air."

Walt sat at the table fiddling with the strap of his dive mask "All right," he replied in a disinterested voice, not even looking up from his task.

No more than ten seconds later, Walt saw Brock come down the stairs and back in to the galley, holding something in his hand. This time Walt stopped what he was doing, looked up at Brock and quipped, "Wow, you need less air than a dolphin."

"Ha! Ha!" Brock said, "Good one." Holding up the object in his hand, he asked,

"What's this?"

Staring at the plastic freezer bag, Walt shrugged and said, "I don't know. What is it?"

"I was hoping you could tell me. Let's find out." Brock opened the bag and slid the four old pieces of paper that were inside, out onto the table.

Walt picked up and examined each one. Everything was in Spanish. Neither Walt nor Brock knew very much Span-

ish, but Walt thought one of the papers might be a manifest. He had no idea what the other two were. The fourth
piece of paper was a map, of that Walt was certain. "Where
did you get this?"

Gesturing with his thumb, Brock said, "I found it lying
on the deck, right beside the tarp we used to cover the kayaks."

Walt studied the papers a little longer, before standing
up and saying, "I'll be right back. I'm going to see if Denny
knows anything about this." He left the galley taking the
stairs two at a time. Opening the door to the wheelhouse,
Walt called out, "Hey Denny, we need you down here." Not
waiting for an answer, Walt closed the door and returned
to the galley.

Walt sat down at the table again. After a long pause, he
said, "Hollis."

"Huh?" Brock grunted, still examining the map.

"I'll bet Hollis planted this as a joke." Walt said as he
heard the engine noise diminish and felt the momentum
slow.

Brock shrugged, "Maybe."

A moment later, Denny came into the room. He walked
over to the table and picked up one of the papers. "What is
this?"

"We don't know," Walt answered. "Brock found it out
on the rear deck."

Denny's brow wrinkled and he looked confused, "Who
do they belong to?"

"They belong to me."

Everyone turned and stared, surprised at seeing a figure in the doorway. A woman, standing straight with her shoulders square, stood at the entrance to the galley. She wore a blue windbreaker jacket and tan pants. The blue baseball cap covering her head was soaked, along with the rest of her clothes. Water dripped from her auburn hair. The three men continued to gape, dumbfounded.

At last, Brock spoke up, "Who the hell are you?"

"I am Captain Lynn Meyers," she said, pointing to the papers lying on the table, "and *that* is my property."

Chapter Six

Ten a.m. found the three men standing around on the stern deck of the *Hunkered Down*. The rain had stopped, but the sky was still dark and gray. The sea remained choppy and a stiff, warm breeze blew from the southwest. The boat lay at anchor in forty-two feet of water to keep from drifting too far off course.

For the past hour, the men had listened to the surreal story Captain Meyers had spun. She had told them about the Cubans on the raft. She explained how the old man gave her the packet and what he said. She mentioned the note pad in little Lolita's duffel bag which had the names and addresses of her relatives living in Miami. The Captain told the men everything she could remember, leaving out nothing. Lynn Meyers sat at the Galley table, wrapped in a wool blanket as she told the tale.

While she took a hot shower, Walt, Brock and Denny pondered her story.

Brock asked, "What do you think, Walt?"

"I'm not sure. Her story explains what I saw on her boat

last night."

"What did you see on what boat?"

"The *Lit'l Lynny*. She was moored next to the *Hunkered Down*. I took a walk along the dock last night and I noticed the fishing deck of the *Lit'l Lynny* was askew. When I came back, I saw two men walking away from her. At the time, it didn't seem like a big deal, but it makes sense now."

Denny spoke up, "Don't tell me you believe her."

"Like I said, I'm not sure."

Brock said, "Neither am I. Some parts of her story seem far-fetched, but it's also hard to imagine that she made all that up."

"And then there's the map and the log," said Walt, as if trying to add up the positives.

"You guys sound crazy!" exclaimed Denny. "We need to take her ashore and let the proper authorities handle this situation."

"What if it is real?" Brock asked, with a faraway look in his eyes.

Walt said in a low, wishful tone, "I'd sure like to get a good look at that log."

"You don't even read Spanish," Denny said.

"We could get the Captain to interpret it for us, she speaks and reads Spanish."

Cocking his head, Denny fixed Walt with a skeptical stare.

"Could be worth tens, maybe even hundreds of millions of dollars," said Brock, still in a state of abstraction.

Agitated, Denny said, "Could be this, could be that. I

know one thing for certain, that woman is trouble."

"And I know you only get one or two great opportunities in a lifetime," Brock added.

"All right," Walt interjected, "here's what I think. We'll go back in there; she should be out of the shower by now. We'll ask more questions, take a good look at the map and the other papers, and decide what we're going to do. If all three of us don't believe her, we'll call the Coast Guard and head for shore. Should we have a split decision, we'll call Hollis. He can come and pick up whoever wants out and the other or others can continue on." After a brief pause, he continued, "If all three of us want to go on, I guess we go and search for sunken treasure." Walt paused once more before asking, "Brock?"

"Sounds like a plan."

"Denny?"

"All right, but if I don't like what I see or hear, I'm gone. No hard feelings."

"That's it then, let's go."

As the men started for the galley, Brock put his arm around Denny's shoulder and smiled. He said, "C'mon buddy, like Walt always says, you gotta die of something."

Entering the galley one by one, the men found their female passenger seated at the far end of the table, cradling a steaming cup of black coffee. Her wet auburn hair hung loosely around her shoulders. She wore the clothing Walt had set out for her, a gray sweatshirt, tan cargo pants and white socks. The sweatshirt was tucked in at the waist to keep the pants from sliding down. She had the pant legs rolled up to keep from tripping over them. Lynn Meyers wore no make-up and her freshly scrubbed face gave her an outdoorsy, healthy appearance.

Walt took the seat to Lynn's right, Brock to her left and Denny sat at the opposite end of the table.

Walt acted in a polite manner and said, "Captain Meyers, I hope you don't mind, we have some more questions."

"I feel like I'm in a police interrogation room." she replied, with a nervous edge to her voice. "I guess I can't blame you after I stowed away on your boat and told you my fantastic tale."

"Let's go over it again," Walt said. "You believe the contents of the package are authentic?"

"Yes, I do."

"And this package contains a map, a journal of some kind and a ship's manifest."

"That's right."

"No offense, but this was given to you by a dying man on a raft. He was a stranger to you. How do you know it's not phony?"

"I wouldn't know or even think it's original, except for the fact that folk have been following that package from Cuba, and have killed for it, here and in Cuba."

"And in Cuba?" Denny asked. "You told us about finding your mate dead, but what do you know about Cuba?"

"Just a while ago, while I was in the shower, it clicked. The little Cuban girl, Lolita, told me that her mother died before she could even remember her. She had lived her entire life with her father who never remarried. She said her father was a mechanic and one day when he returned home from work, two men came and took him away. At the time, I assumed the men were government officials, but now I recall Lolita saying the men spoke a funny language. She also said one of the men was very dark, with long, black curly hair and funny drawings on his face."

"Tattoos?" Denny asked.

"Possibly. I would wager not many Cuban officials fit that description. I also think the same man has been following me. I saw a dark-skinned man with long black hair, hanging around the harbor where I keep my boat."

Walt thought of the Maori who worked as Haggarty's mate. He wondered if this could be the same man.

Lynn sipped her coffee before continuing, "Lolita told me that, after two days, when her father didn't return, she walked three hours to her grandfather's house. The grandfather, who lived alone on a small farm close to Pinar del Rio at the North-West end of the island, put her up with the neighbors and went away for a few days. When he returned, he told Lolita her father was in heaven and they must leave right away. That very day he built a raft and gathered some supplies. After dark, they set off. How they got past the authorities is sketchy. Lolita is only twelve years old. She doesn't even know or understand everything that has happened."

"What a sad story." Brock said, going to the counter and pouring himself a cup of coffee.

Lynn said, "Yes, it is. On the voyage, Lolita's grandfather told her they were going to live with her aunt and uncle in the United States. He said the package had been handed down through their family from generation to generation. With Lolita living free, he told her, she could be the one to finally find the treasure of the Santa Luala."

Filling his own cup, and then the cups of the others with coffee, Brock returned to his seat at the table. "So, Lolita is with her relatives, you have the map, and you believe you're being followed."

"That's about the size of things. I'm sure you guys don't trust me yet. I don't know if I can trust you, but I don't have many options."

Walt asked, "Why not turn this over to the police?"

The question was directed at Lynn, but Denny answered, "Turning this over to the police wouldn't work."

Astonishment filled the faces of both Walt and Brock as they turned their heads and stared toward Denny at the same time.

"These are very resourceful people," Denny continued. "They would find Captain Meyers before the police found them. Eventually, she'd crack. They'd have the map and the Captain would be dead."

"But why not give the map to the police?" asked Brock.

Lynn answered this time, "Sooner or later someone is going to mount an expedition. The killers will be waiting and the result will be the same."

"What you're saying is you want to find this shipwreck before they know where you are," said Walt.

"Exactly. After the treasure is discovered and made public, the killers would have a difficult time doing anything about it," Lynn said, watching Walt get up and gaze out of one of the portholes of the galley. Trying to convince the men, she continued, "When I found Charlie dead, I went to my boat and got out to sea as fast as I could. I was fearful that if I reported the crime the killers would get me, either before I got to the police or after I gave an interview. I headed west and stopped for fuel back at the docks where I moored next to your boat.

Last night I was sleeping in my chair in the bridge, when I heard voices. Seeing two men board my boat, I slipped out the side window and crawled over to the *Hunkered Down*, where I hid under a tarp. I only wanted to escape from whoever was after me. I had no plan of asking you for help, but I remembered seeing salvage equipment being loaded aboard your boat yesterday. Hiding under that tarp, I came up with an idea. The four of us could search for the treasure together, whatever we find we split. Lolita gets fifty percent and we'll divide the other fifty percent four ways."

"Sounds like a plan," Brock said, "but we're not equipped for a major salvage operation. We are recreational divers, nothing more."

"So, we search and see what happens. Nothing ventured, nothing gained." Denny stated.

The comment drew incredulous looks once again from Walt and Brock.

Denny raised his hands and asked, in an innocent voice, "What?" Known as a hardcore conservative, Denny was not usually prone to taking chances, especially one with such a high degree of danger.

Shaking his head and chuckling, Walt sat down at the table one more time. After a moment of contemplation, he said, "Let's start by looking at what's in the package."

There would be no need for a vote. The game was on. Like hounds getting their first whiff of their quarry, the men were up for the chase. Walter Ulrich, Brock McGowen, and Dennis Smith, three close friends who were adventurous, amateur treasure hunters, were about to embark on an epic journey.

Had they known the whirlpool of greed, death, and deceit they were being sucked into, their excitement may have been replaced by dread.

Chapter Seven

Lynn deciphered the Spanish document and read aloud, while the men listened intently.

"This is the journal of Benito Hetes, copied in the year 1861 from a copy of the original. This document has been handed down through my family since the year of 1729. Signed, Armando Hetes.

"This is the journal of my voyage aboard the Spanish cargo ship the Santa Luala as documented by Benito Hetes. In the year 1717, I was hired on as a cook's mate aboard the Santa Luala. We were part of a fleet of thirty-eight ships, which set sail in May from Havana bound for Madrid, Spain. Each of the thirty-eight ships was loaded with valuables. The list of items aboard the Santa Luala is described in the manifest.

"On the first night, a mighty storm came upon us. Our ship became separated from the fleet. At dawn the following morning, the Captain ordered the crew to sail the Santa Luala away from the storm. For two days, we sailed west, fighting the storm. By the time the skies cleared our ship was badly beaten. The mast was broken off and she was taking on water. We tried to limp back to Havana, but a second storm hit. This storm was not as fierce as the first, but the ship was in poor condition. The horrendous wind and seas pushed us farther to the west. On the fifth night, just after dark, the Santa Luala floundered and went under.

"I escaped and floated on a hatch cover prior to washing up on a small Cay. I believed myself to be the only survivor until a Spanish officer washed ashore. His name was Alvereze. Mr. Alvereze had been a junior officer aboard the ship. He was a decent man, and very resourceful.

"Much debris had washed ashore. We used a small section of canvas sail, stretched between two shrubs to catch rainwater. We caught fish almost every day for food. After three months of not seeing any ships, we decided to take our chances on the open ocean. I was not a sailor and was not eager to be out to sea again, but officer Alvereze believed that we would die of some terrible tropical disease long before help would come.

"Using the wreckage of the Santa Luala, we built a small sailing raft. For many days and nights, we sailed east. Officer Alvereze navigated by the sun and stars. Our skin became so burned by the sun, it blistered, peeled away, and blistered again. At last, we reached land on the Peninsula De Guana Hacabbes Cuba. I returned to my family farm at Pinar Del Rio. I do not know whatever became of officer Alvereze, but I presume he returned to Havana."

Lynn stopped reading, looked at the men, and said, "The next entry is dated 1720." She began to read once more.

"Since my return, three years ago, from my voyage on the Santa Luala, I have never desired to travel the oceans again. I have wondered about the cargo that went down with the ship. Many inquiries have been made, but I have found no record of an excursion to recover her valuable cargo. I do believe the cargo is still lying where it went down. Furthermore, I believe those riches belong to the people of the land, not to the king of Spain. I intend to one day recover the riches and claim them for my family. It's signed Benito Hetes," Lynn continued, "The next entry is dated 1727. I have spent nearly ten years hoping to find the means to recover the cargo of the Santa Luala. My health being poor, I fear this will not be possible. Should I pass on, my hope is, my family will find this journal so that they may someday recover the gold and silver, which lies at the bottom of the sea. To my knowledge, the Spanish have mounted no expedition. Signed once more by Benito Hetes." Lynn finished reading, set the papers on the table, and said, "That's all."

After a long pause, Walt said, "I don't know, it sounds authentic, but it seems strange that an eighteenth century Cuban farmer would've had such writing skills."

"Good point," Brock said. "I never thought of that. However, the fact that the guy could read and write doesn't mean this is a fake. We have no way of telling for certain."

Denny spoke next, "Let's have a look at one of the other items."

Lynn carefully picked another piece of very old paper up

from the tabletop, and started reading, "This is a copy of the manifest of the Santa Luala. The document washed ashore on the small island where I was temporarily stranded. Benito Hetes, 1717. The first items listed are food and supplies for the voyage," Lynn said, skimming through the manifest. "Here is where it gets to the cargo. One thousand two hundred gold bars, Three thousand, three hundred and sixty silver bars, five hundred thousand gold cobs."

"What is a cob?" Brock wondered.

"Cob was the term used for coin. Most cobs had the seal of the King of Spain stamped on them or sometimes a stamp indicating the area from where they'd been minted."

"You know your treasure."

"I guess it comes from living in Florida and working at sea. There is so much treasure, so close by at all times, it's hard not to know something about it," Lynn said. "The problem is finding it." She paused before continuing, "Let's see what else is here. One hundred and fifty-seven lengths of gold chain, although it doesn't say how long the lengths are, various jewels and jewelry and one thousand four hundred silver cobs." Reading the last item, Lynn said, "That is some remarkable treasure."

"Yes, it'd be astonishing if it's still down there, and if we could find it," Denny added.

Walt said, "How about the map? Maybe we can pinpoint the location of the shipwreck. Captain Meyers, did you go over the map yet?"

"Yes, I did," Lynn replied, unfolding the map. Pointing to an Island marked Cuba, she went on, "Here is Cuba."

Tracing her finger along spots drawn on the map, "These must be the Keys, and I'm certain this one is Key West."

Walt tapped his finger on an x drawn on the map, stating, "Surely this x marks the wreck. If so, the Santa Luala appears to be very close to a small Island."

"You're right. I checked the charts and that area is dotted with small, uninhabited Islands. The one closest to the x is Summers Cay. The waters are shallow and the currents aren't too strong." After a short pause, Lynn stated, "That's it. That's all I have."

Turning to Denny, Walt asked, "Do you have anything that could give us a better description of the area?"

Denny rubbed his sandy hair in thought. He said, "I just might ... give me a minute." He rose and left the galley, climbing the stairs to the wheelhouse.

Brock, who had been quiet for a while, shifted his bulky frame in his chair at the table and said, "I don't understand why the Spanish wouldn't recover a valuable treasure such as this."

"That, I can't answer," Lynn replied.

"Walt, you've researched the subject more than I have, do you recall anything about the wreck of the Santa Luala?" Brock asked.

Walt had spent more than a few hours reading up about Spanish Galleons and shipwrecks. "No, I don't recall anything however; it would take more time than I have to go over everything documented on the Spanish treasure fleet. The story sounds authentic, but it is hard to tell. I do know that Havana was a stopping point for many Spanish Galleons coming from South America on their way to Spain. When ships went down with no survivors, the location of the wreck was difficult to pinpoint. Usually when there were survivors, the Spanish would salvage the cargo, especially when a ship went down in shallow water. The salvage operations were well documented. You could almost call them famous. Why there's not a famous story of the Santa Luala is a mystery. Maybe something happened to the Spanish officer."

At that moment, Denny entered the galley carrying a small blue book in his right hand. "Got it," he said, opening the book on the table. "This book describes all of the islands in this area. Summers Cay is a small atoll a quarter mile long by one hundred yards wide at its widest spot."

"Does the book give the coordinates?" Walt asked.

"Sure does."

With a nod and a slight smile Walt asked, "In that case, what are we waiting for?"

———————

The Florida Keys consists of over 1,700 islands. Most of the islands are uninhabitable and unnamed. Summers Cay was located approximately twenty-six miles from their current position. Denny piloted the boat with Captain Lynn Meyers by his side providing company and giving pointers. The trip did not take long. While en-route, Walt and Brock readied the scuba gear they had rented from a trusted dive shop back on Key West.

Walt entered the water feet first with barely a splash. Dawn had broken clear and now at 9 a.m., the eastern sun shone bright. The sea was dead calm. Reflections of the sun's rays looked like mercury shimmying on the surface.

Once they had arrived at what they thought was the spot the wreck was situated they had decided that it was too late to dive that day and after an evening of talk about lost treasure and the luxuries they could buy with their share, they had all departed to sleep.

The air temperature was already in the high eighties and Walt had been sweating under his wet suit. He enjoyed being in the water, which was a few degrees cooler. As he cleared his mouthpiece, Walt held one hand over his eyes to cut the glare and watched Brock's flamboyant back flip over the *Hunkered Down's* side. The splash caused by Brock hitting the water, rained over Walt. He had to give a few flipper kicks to maintain his position against the waves created by Brock's inelegant entrance.

When Brock came up, the two men trod water until they readied their dive equipment.

At last, Walt slipped his mask down over his eyes and asked, "Are you ready to go diving, partner?"

"I'm ready to get rich!" Brock enthusiastically replied.

Denny leaned against the stern of the boat as he called down to the men in the water, "Stick to the plan. Don't take any chances."

"Yes, Mother," Brock replied with a roll of his eyes.

Denny shook his head and spat, "Smart ass." However, he could not hold back a smile.

Walt gave Denny a wink and Brock the thumbs up and both men dove for the bottom.

The plan devised to find the wreck of the *Santa Luala* called for two dives per day. Walt and Brock would do the diving, using the grid search method. They would cordon off a square section of bottom using rope and underwater buoys. Walt and Brock would then search every inch of sea floor within the grid using an underwater metal detector. The metal detector looked like those used on dry land by amateur treasure hunters. The type Walt and Brock used on this trip employed pulse induction. Pulse induction models were specifically designed for use in saltwater. If they found anything, they would mark it with a pinger. The pinger sent a signal to a receiver on board the boat, making the location easy to find. The divers planned to search one grid in the morning and one in the afternoon. Denny and Lynn would remain aboard the boat and take care of everything top side.

For three days, the routine had been the same. Walt and Brock dove in the morning and searched one grid. At midday, they took a break for a rest and a light lunch. They spent their afternoons diving once again and searching a second grid. So far, their searching was in vain.

Three days.

Six grids.

Nothing.

The evening of the third day found Walt and Brock sitting on the stern deck, having a beer, their first since they had left land. The air temperature was eighty-eight degrees and the humidity was high. Both men wore no shirts or shoes, only shorts.

Brock held his half-full, sweating bottle of beer against the side of his face and said, "Nothing against Denny, he's a good cook, but I'm in favor of Captain Meyers doing the cooking more often."

"Yea, that sounds good to me too. I'm delighted that she took a turn in the galley tonight. That pot roast was terrific."

The friends finished their beers in silence, watching the fiery red ball of the sun sink below the horizon. Walt reached into the small cooler of beer on ice and lifted two more bottles out. He handed one bottle to Brock. Opening his own bottle, Walt said, "Let's take a break tomorrow. We'll make a dive in the morning and take the afternoon and maybe the next day off."

"Sounds great, this searching is hard work."

"After a short break, we can go back at it once again," Walt agreed. "But," he continued with a slight grin and a motion of his head, "They may not enjoy our company."

Brock's gaze followed in the direction Walt had motioned. He saw Denny and Lynn sitting on the bow of the *Hunkered Down.* Lynn was sitting close to Denny, talking and laughing as if telling a story. Denny was staring straight at her and grinning like the Cheshire Cat. Brock furled his brow, "What? You mean Denny and the Captain ... no. Do you think so?"

Walt shrugged and said, "I don't know, it seems that way to me. They look like they really enjoy each other's company"

Brock watched the couple for a full minute. "Why am I always the last to know these things?"

Walt chuckled and said, "Because you're a big oaf. Now stop staring."

The men drank their beer. Walt changed the subject to fishing. As he and Brock talked idly about a tuna-fishing trip they had made a few years ago, Walt's mind was on his earlier comments. He was one hundred percent certain about Denny and Lynn. Denny had always been a polite gentleman in the company of women. He was reserved, maybe even shy. Walt noticed how Denny spoke freely and comfortably when he was around Lynn. He also noticed how Lynn looked at Denny when he did not know she was watching.

They were spending four to five hours a day alone with each other while Walt and Brock dove. That was plenty of time for them to get to know each other. A man and a woman with mutual interests becoming close seemed natural. Good for them, Walt thought as he sipped his beer in toast to the pair. Good for them.

Chapter Eight

That night Walt decided to sleep out on the stern deck under the stars. He took a pillow and light blanket from his bunk out to the deck. A warm breeze wafted across the deck. Lying on the deck, Walt felt the minor rocking motion of the boat as the gentle waves caressed her hull. The clear night offered a panoramic view. The constellations appeared in plain sight. Walt wished that he knew what more of them were. There were the Big and Little Dippers, the Seven Sisters and the Southern Cross, but that was the extent of Walt's knowledge. Other constellations were visible, though Walt had no idea of which ones they were. He noticed heavenly bodies that he thought must be planets, but he was not sure.

As he lay flat on his back with his head on the pillow, Walt made up his mind to learn the stars. Next year he would impress his friends by using a sexton to navigate by the sun and stars. Next year. What if there was no next year? What would happen if they found this Treasure? Walt allowed himself to fantasize. If they located this shipwreck, they would be able to take year-long vacations.

While Walt made a six-figure income, he still had to live by someone else's rules. The discovery of a treasure this size would mean he would no longer have a job dictating his life. No more worrying about more bills to pay. Walt also made a mental list of the people that he could help. Money could do many good things for many people. He never thought about the actual treasure. Walt had no visions of shiny gold doubloons. That may have been important to a historian, but it meant nothing to Walt. As he drifted off to sleep, Walt's thoughts were of the life money could provide, not the money itself. In the deep of the night, his dreams depicted exotic islands, exploration and adventure.

The sun shone bright the next morning. Sparkling blue water, the ocean breeze and the taste of salt in Walt's mouth all added to the atmosphere of living at sea. Walt and Brock decided to dive without their wetsuits. They were making only one dive today and the warm eighty-two-degree water felt refreshing against their skin. Wearing swim trunks, fins and their scuba gear, they set about marking off the grid area they wanted to search on this dive. This was a familiar routine by now and the two men finished in less than ten minutes.

Brock started searching the far end of the grid. Holding the underwater metal detector just above the bottom, he kicked his fins and drifted along little by little. The clear water provided good visibility out to forty yards. Walt watched a small shark swim right outside the perimeter of the grid. He could see the light color on the tip of the shark's fins. Walt did not consider himself an expert, but he recognized the small animal as a Reef Shark.

Reef sharks are not normally aggressive and this one was no more than three feet in length, so Walt had little to fear. He remained cautious, however. Not wanting to turn his back on the shark, he watched it circle once and then swim away. He continued to inspect his surroundings for several moments after the shark disappeared into the gloom. Walt loved the peace and quiet he found underwater. He also loved the feeling of weightlessness diving provided. Scuba diving brought a sense of joy unmatched by any other activity he'd found.

When the shark did not return, Walt turned to the grid to begin his search. That's when he saw it. His eyes grew wide and he tilted his head forward. He felt that his mind was having trouble registering what his eyes saw. Squinting, Walt backed away with one sweep of his fins. Exhaling a great breath, he stared at an object rising from the bottom. The air bubbles from his breath rose in front of his mask, distorting his view. When his vision cleared, Walt ogled the article.

As he regained his wits, Walt knew what he had seen. A person who had never seen the ocean, or even a ship, would know what this was. Even someone from Kansas would recognize this object, Walt thought. It was an anchor. He began to circle, with his eyes remaining locked on the discovery. The main shaft was as long as Walt and a prong on either side curved along the seabed. Although barnacles and other living and dead plant life covered the object, he easily discerned the familiar shape.

Fascinated, he wondered how he could not have noticed this earlier. Walt switched on the metal detector and ran it over the object. The signal confirmed the presence of metal underneath the crust of sea life. Glancing in the direction of Brock, Walt noticed the other diver motioning wildly, trying to get his attention.

Brock indicated that he wanted Walt to come to him.

As Walt swam towards his friend, the metal detector signaled a few times, but he continued at a fast pace. When he reached Brock, he came to a stop and hovered in front of him.

Brock was smiling around his mouthpiece. In each of his hands, he held an object. Both objects were covered with the same crust, though not as thick, as the anchor. The object in Brock's right hand was the size and shape of a pencil. His left hand held something a bit longer and wider.

Walt pointed up and saw his partner nod in understanding.

Together the two men kicked for the surface. They emerged simultaneously forty yards from the *Hunkered Down.*

Brock spat out his mouthpiece and let out a loud "Whoop!" In between gasps of air he blurted out, "This is it buddy. There's a wreck down there."

His friend's excitement was contagious and Walt could

not help smiling. "The anchor is on the other side of the grid."

Brock gaped at Walt, his eyes grew even wider, "Woo Hoo!" he exclaimed, before getting a mouth full of salt water down his lungs.

Walt's smile turned in to a laugh as Brock coughed, laughing and sputtering. Giving Brock a pat on the back, he motioned towards the boat and said, "C'mon pal, let's go tell the others."

Lynn Meyers stood leaning on the stern gunwale as the two men reached the boat. "What's going on?" she asked, watching Walt hoist himself up the boarding ladder.

Brock followed and as he hopped from the ladder to the deck he coughed and said, "He tried to drown me."

Walt grunted a short laugh and added, "We found a wreck."

At the same time, both men noticed the look of concern in Lynn's eyes. The mood changed instantly. "What's going on up here?" Walt asked.

Lynn pointed to the west and replied, "We've got company."

Turning in the direction that Lynn was pointing, Walt placed his right hand over his brow. He flexed his knees to steady himself on the rocking boat, the way that only those who are comfortable and used to being at sea do. The shade his hand provided was slight and Walt had to squint to see.

Surreal was the word that came to mind as Walt stared at the scene before him. The picture of Denny standing along the port rail looking through a pair of binoculars seemed like something out of a travel brochure.

Since the trip began, Walt and Brock had gotten some sun lounging on the deck between dives. The time the men spent diving had not allowed for too deep of a tan. Lynn had spent all her thirty-six years under the southern sun. She had a permanent light tan and kept covered up most of the time to protect her fair skin.

Denny however, looked like a sun god. His sandy hair had turned three shades lighter. A pair of blue board shorts was all he wore. His normally pale skin had a deep dark tan the color of rich, stained mahogany.

Denny was not the focal point of the scene, however. The picture Walt saw was Denny set against the deep blue of the Gulf waters and the lighter blue of the sky. Wisps of white clouds floated here and there against the azure. The sun shone bright. A mile off in the background rested a large, black, sailing ship. Darker, more ominous blue-black skies of a thunderstorm passing along the distant horizon framed the vessel.

Walt removed his scuba gear and stepped up alongside Denny. In a serious voice, he asked, "How long has that been there?"

Denny's eyes never left the ship. "I noticed her coming in under full sail right after you went down. She ferruled her sails and has been at anchor for about fifteen minutes now." Handing the binoculars to Walt, he added, "She's nice, isn't she?"

"Yep, she's a beauty." From what Walt could see, he thought the entire vessel was jet black. From her sleek fiberglass hull, to her graphite composite mast, everything appeared to be black. At this distance, even the sheets looked black.

"She smells of money."

Nodding, Walt agreed. Even from over one mile away, he could distinguish her delicate lines and sweeping sailing curves.

Without speaking, they stood, staring at the vessel for a few moments. Neither man noticed Brock standing behind them. "Are you fellows going to stand around gawking at that black dinghy all day?"

"What do you make of her?" Denny asked.

"Who cares? We found a wreck. We're rich." Brock said in a nonchalant tone.

Turning to face Brock, Denny asked, "Are you serious?" Brock's enormous smile told Denny he was. Sneaking a glance at Walt, Denny saw him frown.

"We found a wreck, but we're not rich yet."

"Not yet," Brock repeated.

"Brock, you don't even know what's down there."

"Not yet." Brock's smile would not go away.

Denny asked, "What did you find?"

Brock spoke fast. All traces of a nonchalant tone disappeared, "We found a wreck. We found THE wreck, the *Santa Luala.* Like I told you, we are rich. Congratulations Denny, it couldn't have happened to a nicer guy. You like that black boat? Why don't you see what the owner wants for it?"

"Easy big fellow," Walt said.

"Hey Walt, if you want to be negative about this, be my guest. I believe in positive thinking and I'm positive we're rich."

Walt found it impossible not to get caught up in Brock's enthusiasm. He started laughing. So did Denny. Brock joined in and laughed the loudest and hardest.

Walt knew his friend well. Brock was excited, his adrenaline was pumping, but his rant was all in fun. Brock was an intelligent man Walt knew, and he was not naïve enough to believe that this excursion would be simple.

While the divers filled Denny in on their discovery, Lynn filled a large sealable drum with seawater. Inside, she placed the objects Brock had found.

The group talked things over and decided that even though they had not seen any movement from the black sailing vessel, under the circumstances it would be wise for Lynn to keep a low profile. She went below and fixed a premature lunch. When she returned with a tray of chicken salad sandwiches, she was wearing baggy cotton pants and a long-sleeved shirt. She had her hair tucked up under her long-billed hat. Someone would have to have very good optics or get very close to recognize Lynn, or even know she was female.

Changing their plan for one lone dive today was simple. Everyone was anxious to find out what else was down there, waiting to be found. As soon as possible Walt and Brock would make another excursion to the floor of the sea. Becoming caught up in the excitement, Denny wanted to go down with them. Walt talked him out of the idea, not wanting to leave Lynn topside alone. Not while the mysterious black boat was hanging around.

Chapter Nine

Warm tropical sunlight shone down on the crew of the *Hunkered Down.* The men wore nothing but the swim trunks they dove in and sunglasses. Denny was still clad in his board shorts. Walt readied the scuba gear for another dive. He replaced the partially spent air tanks with full ones. Brock and Denny went to work on the objects brought up from the sea floor. They each kept a casual eye on the ship anchored off their port rail. The storm passed seven miles out on the horizon without ever threatening the boat or her occupants.

"This one looks like a knife to me," Brock announced, squinting as he held the larger object up to the sun.

Denny chipped away at the smaller object with a small hammer. Upon hearing Brock's comment, he paused and said, "I doubt it. The steel used in the fifteenth and sixteenth centuries would've depreciated to nothing by now."

"But Walt found an anchor."

"He said the metal detector showed faint traces of metal. I'd guess the item that's there now is mostly made up of coral, barnacles, and the likes. The iron deteriorated and the sea life built up over the centuries, like the way reefs are formed."

"Well this is made of some kind of metal. Who wants a stupid knife anyway?"

"Maybe it's gold. I don't think gold ever deteriorates."

"Hey, maybe it's a gold knife."

With a shake of his head, Denny chuckled and went back to chipping with the hammer.

Removing the buildup was a long, slow process. The work was delicate. The men had to be careful not to damage anything of value.

At noon, Lynn served fish cakes that she whipped up herself and a garden salad. After lunch, they went back to work. They wore sunglasses and worked shirtless in the heat of the day.

In the middle of the afternoon, they were hard at it when Walt heard a distant sound. He licked his lips removing the salt.

"I think our neighbors are coming to pay us a visit."

Everyone looked toward the mysterious black sailing vessel. Her sails remained furled and she appeared to be lying at anchor. Coming across the expanse of ocean between the *Hunkered Down* and the black boat, were two small speedboats.

Brock and Denny dropped the objects and their tools into the barrel and threw a tarp over it.

"I think you'd better go below," Denny told Lynn.

"All right, but you guys be careful," Lynn directed her

reply at all three of the men, but her eyes remained locked on Denny. She hurried below and gathered up the information the old Cuban had given her. She stuffed the map, the log and the manifest into the plastic packet. Wrapping the packet in a blanket, she hid the it under the galley stove.

Lynn went to a porthole and looked out. She kept her face away from the glass, staying a step back. She could see out, but she knew it would be hard for anyone to see her.

Brock grabbed a six-foot gig and laid it on the deck at his feet. The gig had a wooden handle and three sharp, steel prongs on the tip. Normally used for fishing, Brock knew the gig would make a lethal weapon, should he need it.

Each of the men tucked a sheathed knife into the waistband in the back of their shorts. Walt put a spear into the spear gun and cocked it. He set the spear gun along the gunwale, out of sight, but nearby. The men were not looking for a fight. However, on the open ocean it was always wise to be prepared, especially with Captain Meyers aboard.

Watching the speedboats close the distance, Walt said, "No matter what, they're not coming aboard."

"Right," Denny agreed.

"You got it," Brock added.

The speedboats throttled down as they came alongside the *Hunkered Down.* They were small, fast craft with large inboard engines. The engines purred and sounded smooth. Black fiberglass made up the hull of the speedboats. Each boat could seat four passengers. The first craft held two men, while the second had one.

All three of the men in the speedboats had black hair. Their skin was the color of coffee. The man at the controls of the first boat was huge. He had a square face and shoulder length hair. Standing almost seven feet tall and weighing maybe three hundred pounds, he was an imposing sight.

Sitting in the passenger seat was a man of average height and weight. He had shorter hair, which he wore slicked back, and a thin mustache. The operators of the boats pulled alongside leaving the engines idling. As the boats drifted to a stop, this man stood and waved a greeting, "Hail the *Hunkered Down.*" He spoke English with a heavy accent.

"Hello," Walt answered. "What can we do for you?"

"We have come to extend an invitation. Our Captain, Juan Chavez, invites you to dine with him aboard his vessel, the *Searcher.*"

While this man spoke, the man in the second boat shut off the engine and threw a bowline over the rail of the *Hunkered Down.* Brock grabbed the line and tied it fast to the port rail. The man then jumped from the boat he was in, to the other speedboat.

"Dinner will be served at eight," the man with the thin mustache continued. "The Captain will expect you at seven. You may use our boat for your arrival."

Not waiting for a reply, the large man at the controls gunned the engine. The speedboat shot away in the direction of the black ship.

"So, what are you going to do?" Lynn asked, after the men told her of the invitation.

Everyone sat around the table in the galley, except Walt. He stood by the porthole and stared at the black ship. "I think we should accept the invitation."

"No way," Denny said.

Brock chided, "Come on Denny, lighten up. How are you going to buy that boat if you don't meet the owner?"

"We won't buy anything if we're dead," Denny snapped.

"Wait, I'm serious," Walt said. "We have their speed-boat. If we don't show for dinner, they'll come over here again to get it back. As far as we know, no one knows of Captain Meyers being aboard. She can stay here out of sight. Why don't we go and meet this Juan Chavez? We'll give him our 'we're on vacation, nothing more' story, and no one will be the wiser. He'll never know the Captain is aboard or what we're doing here."

Brock said, "You know Walt, the more you hang out with me, the smarter you get."

Lynn spoke next, "I have to admit, that sounds like a good scheme, if you're good actors."

"My middle name is Tom Hanks," Brock replied, "Brock, Tom Hanks, McGowen, that's me."

Lynn could not help laughing. She said, "You seem more like Gary Busey."

This comment made everyone laugh. Everyone except Denny. He had a worried look on his face.

Walt noticed Denny's concern and asked, "What do you say Denny? You decide, do we go or not?"

"I don't relish the thought of having dinner with strangers, but we don't have many choices. They'd get suspicious if we don't show up. I guess the best thing to do would be to go."

———

Singing as it left Brock's hand, the bowline sailed over the rail of the black ship. A crewmember gathered up the line and tied it off. At five minutes to seven, Walt, Brock, and Denny climbed the boarding ladder to the deck of the *Searcher.* Walt wore a linen shirt, and casual trousers. He was dressed much the same as the other two.

Six crewmembers met them on the deck. Standing in two rows, three to a row, were four men and two petite women. Walt recognized the man with the thin mustache from the speedboat as one member of the greeting party. The man was smiling, as were all the crewmembers. He nodded his head as Walt's eyes caught his own.

The crew was dressed impeccably in white navel type uniforms. Each of the crew had olive skin and dark hair and the women were very pretty. At the head of the two rows was a tall man dressed in black. He wore knee length black boots, black slacks and a silk shirt with baggy sleeves. A mustache and pointed goatee adorned his face and he wore his wavy dark hair combed back. The first signs of silver streaked his temples, giving the man a distinguished look.

The man's smile however, was bright white and his eyes sparkled with charm.

"Welcome aboard," the man said with genuine friendliness. In a voice accented with Spanish, he introduced himself, "I am Captain Juan Chavez, also known as The Spaniard."

The men shook hands with the Captain in turn, while introducing themselves. Walt had pushed the idea to accept the invitation. Although he had sold the idea to the others, he had felt uneasy about the whole situation. Having met the Captain however, he began to relax and feel pleased that they had accepted.

Brock was in a jovial frame of mind as usual, and asked, "Are you expecting an America's Cup race to pass by?"

"Ha, ha," The Spaniard laughed and replied, "Not at all. You see this vessel was built for travel, not racing. No, we are mere travelers, *Searcher*s."

"What is it you're searching for?"

"The next sunrise. The next uninhabited island. The wonders of the world." The Spaniard said waving an arm at the horizon with a flourish.

As the sun sank low in the western sky, The Spaniard gave the men a tour of his boat. They toured topside first. Each part and fitting was top of the line. The *Searcher* was a well-kept boat. Everything was in its place and the polished Teak decks shined. She was also an expensive boat. The vessel sported every modern design available from composite masts to the sleek lines of her hull.

Under a removable canvas canopy, a twelve-foot circular

sauna sat mid deck in front of a well-stocked entertainment center. The entertainment center consisted of a fifty-two-inch blue ray projection television, CD and DVD players and a computer. Enormous speakers framed the high-tech equipment. An equally well stocked bar occupied one corner of the space. Spacious couches and lounge chairs adorned the other corner. Intimate lighting completed the luxurious atmosphere.

When they reached the bridge, they found it even more impressive. While Brock found the entertainment area to be the coup de grace, Denny found himself in awe on the bridge. Computers monitored and controlled every aspect of the boat. The trimming of the sails was totally automated. The pilot could press one button and the sails would be set. The high-tech system could detect pitch and yaw, and adjust the sails in an instant to maximize the wind. Electronic monitors kept the boat on an even keel. She never listed more than twelve degrees to port or starboard.

The *Searcher* was one of only a handful of sailing boats in the world to have this kind of onboard system. The Spaniard gracefully explained the intricacies of the boat as he led the men to the dining room.

While the rest of the ship employed every modern convenience, the dining room gave the impression of stepping back in time. Walt was amazed as he followed the others into the room. Candle lamps illuminated the fifteen by eighteen-foot room. The floor was smooth polished oak and the walls were made of rough oak plank. The candles emitted a subtle light. There was an antique Mahogany table in the center of the room with eight places set for dinner. A small, silver, engraved candelabrum holding six lit candles formed the centerpiece.

The room itself gave Walt the feeling of time travel, but the decorations were what astonished him most. Antiques from centuries gone by hung from each of the four walls. The ten-foot high ceiling was made up of oak plank supported by large, exposed oak beams. From one of the beams hung a small wooden chest suspended by four hemp ropes.

The lid of the chest was open. Denny walked over and admired the silver coins, which filled the chest to the top. Brock examined the blades that were on display on one of the walls. There were knives of different types, daggers, gullys, marlinspikes and a few boarding axes. Boarding cutlasses with wood handles, brass pommels, and brass hand guards hung from wooden pegs as if ready for use.

Walt moved to his right and stared at the opposite wall. An impressive array of guns adorned this wall. There were wheel lock, matchlock and flintlock muskets. He saw pistols of many sizes and shapes—French pistols, volley pistols with four barrels which all fired at once, Blunderbuss pistols and turn over pistols.

The centerpiece of this display was a boarding Blunderbuss from the 1700's. The scattergun had a seventeen-inch embossed barrel with a two-inch diameter opening and an embossed walnut stock. It looked as though it were brand new. Walt considered himself a history buff when it came to pirates. He read scores of books about adventures on the high seas during the time of privateering and pirates. From what he could see, every piece appeared to be original. Walt imagined the collection must have been very rare and worth a small fortune.

Tucked into one corner of the dining room was a well-stocked bar. The Spaniard stepped behind the bar and took four sifter glasses and a dull white ceramic bottle from a shelf above his head. As he poured three fingers of Jamaican Rum into each glass, he spoke to Walt, "Ah yes, the English Boarding Blunderbuss, not very accurate ... "

"But awfully effective at close range," Walt interjected.

"You know your weapons, Walt."

"I've always been fascinated by the era of the Trade and Treasure fleets."

"You and I have a great deal in common. The exploits accomplished on the world's oceans have enthralled me since childhood."

"Where do you find pieces of this quality?" Walt asked turning back to the wall.

"Some are purchased from dealers, many are discovered."

"From shipwrecks?"

"No. I buy them from private sources." The Spaniard went from man to man, passing out the drinks. "Take these gully knives señor," he said to Brock as he took one from its place on the wall. The knife was plain, with a wooden handle and a six-inch blade. The Spaniard held the knife by the blade and raised it to eye level. "The gully knife was commonly found on sailing vessels. The sailors had many uses for this type of knife, from cutting rope and sails to cutting meat and vegetables."

With a smile and a flick of his wrist, The Spaniard threw the knife into the air. The knife turned end for end, before he caught it by the handle, flipped it over and handed it to Brock handle first. "This particular knife was found along with a horde of other antique seafaring items in an old woman's hay loft near Madrid. How it came to be there has been lost in the passage of time."

"Maybe pirates stashed it there," Brock said, in a casual voice, placing the knife in its original position on the wall.

The Spaniard laughed and raised his glass in toast, "Here is to all the souls who had the courage to roam the seas, even the pirates."

Everyone joined in the toast. Walt and Denny sipped their drinks, The Spaniard and Brock drained their glasses. When Captain Chavez went behind the bar to refill, the door to the dining room opened and a beautiful young woman strolled in. She looked to be in her early twenties with black hair wrapped in a tight bun. The young lady had the same golden-brown skin as The Spaniard and the rest of the crew, and large brown eyes. She wore heels and a short blue evening dress. A couple wearing formal attire followed the woman. The distinguished man and elegant woman appeared to be in their late fifties.

"I just spoke to the cook," the young lady said, in heavily accented English. "He says dinner is finished."

"Ah, Bonita," said the Spaniard, walking over and slipping his arm around her lithe waist. She was very easy on the eyes. "Allow me to make the introductions. My lovely lady friend's name is Bonita. Bonita hails from the Braga region of Northern Portugal. Giving her a light kiss on the cheek, he continued, "Fellow Spaniards Doctor and Mrs. Qeuokas, I'd like you to meet Walt, Denny, and Brock, our neighbors on the ocean."

Introductions and greetings were passed around. The Spaniard fixed his eyes on Denny and asked, "These men are on vacation doing, what was it you said you were doing?"

Denny was taken back a bit, but he quickly recovered and replied, "Oh, we're doing a little diving, some fishing and sea kayaking."

"Drinking beer, being lazy," Brock chimed in, unfazed by the question. "How about you Doctor, what brings you half way around the world?"

Walt smiled to himself. He was always impressed by Brock's ability to come across as a bit harebrained, and yet point a conversation in the direction he wanted it to go.

"My wife and I are also on vacation. We could not resist Señor Chavez's invitation to sail the high seas in search of adventure."

"Indeed. What is life without friends to enjoy it with? I'm sure you men agree," the Spaniard said.

"In all honesty," Brock said, "these guys are like a lost dog, a homely looking one at that. They keep following me around. I'm going to start throwing rocks and sticks at them soon."

Everyone laughed.

Walt, who had been quiet during the conversation asked a question that had been bothering him for the last few minutes, "Excuse me Captain Chavez, but could I use your washroom before dinner?"

"Of course, it is down the companionway, the third door on the right."

Chapter Ten

Walt walked out of the dining room thinking something was up. He had the feeling there was more to the Spaniard than met the eye and thought that a little snooping would not hurt.

The Spaniard had said the head was the third door on the right. Walt reached the first door on the left and turned the latch. It was unlocked. Glancing both ways to make sure he was not seen, Walt opened the door and stepped inside. He did not get very far. With one foot remaining in the companionway and the other through the open door, he froze.

Standing in front of a mirror, a woman was brushing her long, black, silky hair. Her back was to the door and Walt saw that her hair reached to the small of her back. A tiny tattoo of a Spanish Galleon adorned her right shoulder. She had smooth caramel skin and beautiful curves. Walt had an unobstructed view of her curves, for she was totally naked. Through her reflection in the mirror, Walt noticed her eyes lock on his own. The hairbrush stopped midstroke.

"Oh ... I ... I was looking for the men's room," Walt stammered, feeling his face heat up. He could almost feel his cheeks turning red.

The woman appeared to be about thirty-years of age and she was gorgeous. Before he could make a move to leave the room, she turned around. Still making no effort to conceal herself, the woman spoke with a heavy Spanish accent, "You must be one of our guests for dinner?"

"Ah ... yes and I apologize. I had no idea The Spaniard was married," Walt said, embarrassed beyond belief.

The woman laughed and then said, "I am not The Spaniard's wife. I am Maria Chavez. I am his sister."

"Again, my apologies," Walt said, attempting to keep his eyes on her eyes. The encounter ended Walt's excursion of the boat. He lowered his eyes to stare at the floor and backed out of the room while apologizing again. Walt returned to the dining room just as everyone gathered at the dining table. The Spaniard sat at the head of the table, Bonita at the other end. The Doctor and his wife sat on one side and Walt, Denny and Brock were on the other.

Two waiters entered and poured Spanish Montastrell red wine into antique glass goblets dated from 1761 to 1775 according to The Spaniard. As the waiters served salads to the guests, the dining room door opened and in walked Maria Chavez. She now wore black heels and a black, mid-thigh length, silk dress that showed off her supple body. She wore no makeup Walt noticed, and tiny pearl earrings and a lustrous pearl necklace were her only jewelry.

The Spaniard stood and proclaimed, "Ah Maria, at last. Allow me to make introductions. This is my baby sister Maria, who," he continued with a smile, "always manages to arrive fashionably late."

Maria gave the Doctor and his wife a polite smile as she sauntered by. She stood at her seat, to The Spaniard's right and straight across from Walt.

The Spaniard announced, "These men are Denny, Brock and Walt ... "

Before he could say anything else, Maria, who was staring right through Walt, said, "Yes, Walt and I have already met."

Walt had been flustered when he had walked in on her. However, he was not the type of man to be intimidated by anyone, including a beautiful woman. He rose from his chair, took her hand and brought it to his lips. After placing a lingering kiss on the back of her hand, Walt looked her in the eye and said with a sly grin, "The pleasure was all mine." He expected to detect a slight hint of embarrassment, after all he did see her naked from head to toe. Her reaction surprised Walt.

Maria's eyes sparkled and never left Walt's as she broke into a seductive smile.

A stunned silence came over the room. The Doctor and his wife looked shocked. Denny's eyes widened at the exchange. Brock choked on his wine and almost fell off his chair.

The Spaniard had a look of be wilderment on his face.

His stare went from Walt to Maria. Finding no answers, he said, "Well, why do we not get started with dinner?"

Only then, did Walt let Maria's hand slip from his own. Their eyes remained locked for several more moments.

The meal was a full three courses of traditional Spanish cuisine. Suquet followed the salad. The bowls of Suquet consisted of clams, mussels, two types of fish, squid and shrimp in sauce. The main course was Grouper al la Mallorquina, a dish of Grouper with a variety of vegetables on top. Conversation among the guests was light during dinner. The Spaniard spoke of exotic places he had visited. The Doctor, who was also a pilot, carried on an enthusiastic conversation with Denny. Both men thoroughly enjoyed the talk. Bonita seemed interested in the chitchat, but did not speak. Brock told a few jokes. More than once Walt noticed Maria staring at him. He found it hard to concentrate on anything else. She was stunning. With dinner finished, the crew served Turron, a Spanish almond candy, for desert. Waiters poured glasses of Brandy for after dinner drinks.

After dinner, the Doctor excused himself and his wife and they retired to their cabin. Denny was just about to suggest they should be leaving too, when the Spaniard asked, "So, who is up for a little exercise?"

"What did you have in mind?" Denny asked.

"Wave runners of course. The night is young and life is to be lived." The Spaniard replied in an animated voice. He walked to the bar and pressed a button on an intercom. After a short conversation in Spanish, he released the button and said, "We are all set. What do you say?"

"I'm a good time waiting to happen," Brock replied.

Walt and Denny nodded in agreement.

"Of course, I have but three wave runners so we must double up."

"I had a more relaxing type of exercise in mind." Maria told him, "I believe I will stay on board the *Searcher*. Walt, will you keep me company?"

Again, Maria's comments drew stares from the others. Brock's jaw dropped.

"I'd be happy to," Walt replied.

The Spaniard said, "So it is. Brock, Denny, Bonita my dear, if you will follow me we will hit the water." He opened the door and led them from the room.

Juan Chavez led the group to a large bay one deck below the dining room. Cavernous in appearance, the bay had a high ceiling and was twenty feet by thirty feet. Seawater covered the entire floor of the room. The area had metal catwalks along three of the walls. Tied to the rail of one catwalk, were the black speedboats. A member of the crew stood bent over one of the three wave runners, which were tied to the opposite rail. The man straightened up as they approached and said, "They are ready, Captain."

"Very well," The Spaniard replied. He threw a switch located on a control panel on the wall. In an instant, a large door, which reminded Brock of an electric garage door, began to open. The wave runners floated in four feet of water and when the door opened, the water inside the bay was the same level as the surface of the sea. Night had fallen. From the catwalk, Brock looked out across the ocean. With more than half of its face receiving sunlight, the waxing gibbous moon provided a dusky light.

Walt and Maria leaned on the railing on the stern deck of the boat. They watched as one by one the wave runners shot out of the belly of the *Searcher.* The Spaniard came out first with Bonita clinging to his back. He spun circles and figure eights throwing seawater high into the night sky. Brock and Denny followed suit and soon all three streaked away at break neck speed. Before long, all Walt could see were their headlights. From a distance, they looked like tiny fire flies dancing on the water.

"Very exciting," Maria purred.

"Is the Captain always this adventurous?"

"Of course he is. I believe adventure courses through our veins."

Walt nodded. "It's a good way to go through life, and it seems it's a lifestyle that's paid off for you and your brother. That meal was fit for a king."

Maria smiled in agreement. After a brief pause, she said, "So Walter, tell me about your life,"

"It's not very exciting I'm afraid," Walt said.

"But you're here, on the high seas also living the adventurous life."

Walt smiled. "Yes," he said, "I get to live the dream for a few weeks a year."

Maria said, "Scuba diving, treasure hunting; very exciting business."

Walt felt a charge between them. He leaned in a bit closer and said, "Life is too short."

Maria did not speak. She merely gazed into Walt's eyes.

Walt continued, "What about you? You're here on the ocean on this beautiful evening. You're aboard a world class sailing vessel. You have a flamboyant Captain who's also your brother. Now that sounds like an adventurous life."

Maria said, "Yes, I agree. Life is short, and meant to be lived ... lived with all the life we have flowing in our veins."

Walt smiled and nodded.

Without a word, Maria took her jewelry off. She undid the clasp of her dress and slipped her shoes off. "How about a midnight swim?" She asked, as her dress hit the deck. She wore nothing underneath.

"This is the relaxing exercise you were talking about?"

Maria stepped over the railing and onto the small ledge. Looking back at Walt, she said in a mischievous voice, "No it is not." Turning to face the ocean, she dove into the inky black sea.

While Walt hurried to undress, he could not help thinking that swimming in the open ocean in the middle of the night would be stupidest thing he would ever do, and probably the last. Stepping over the railing, he said aloud, "Oh well, you gotta die of something," and dove in.

The ride back to the *Hunkered Down* was not a long one. The Spaniard had one of his crew take the men back in a large wooden lifeboat. For Walt however, the boat moved in slow motion. He went over the events of the past few hours and tried to make some sense of them. His friends had come back from riding the waves excited, and in good spirits. They trusted The Spaniard, Walt could tell. But, was he a man who *should* be trusted? Walt was not sure. He did like the man, no doubt about that. There was a dashing, debonair style about him. What man doesn't have a young boy's voice inside, wanting to sail the seas and search for adventure?

More questions arose when he turned his thoughts to Maria. He also liked her style. She was comfortable with herself. She was also comfortable with men, as Walt found out while the others were gone. Maria was the type of person who saw something she wanted and she went and got it. No apologies, no excuses, and no regrets. Walt respected that trait. He imagined Maria would do more living in one year than many people do in a lifetime.

The questions were ricocheting in his mind as they reached the *Hunkered Down.* Not knowing if Lynn would even be awake at twelve thirty in the morning, the men were surprised to find her in a frantic state. Fear shone through her eyes as they entered the galley. She was clutching a kitchen knife so tight that her knuckles turned white. In an instant, Lynn relaxed as she recognized her partners.

Denny spoke first, "What's going on?"

"I thought they'd come back."

"Who?"

"The men in the boat." Lynn took a deep breath, as if to steel herself, before continuing, "While you were gone a small boat carrying two men motored up alongside the *Hunkered Down*. I didn't know who they were, but I knew it wasn't you. They were getting ready to come aboard. When I reached for a knife to defend myself, I bumped into the counter. The men must have thought the boat was unoccupied, because when they heard the noise they took off."

"Did you get a good look at them?" Walt asked.

"No, not at all."

"How about lights? Did you see any other boats or lights from boats?"

Lynn shook her head, "I saw some jet skis earlier, but they went in the opposite direction. Besides this was a boat not a jet ski."

Brock said, "That was us on the jet skis."

"How long ago did this happen?" Walt asked.

"About two hours."

Brock turned to Walt and asked, "Do you think the boat came from *Searcher*?"

"No. I would have noticed it."

Lynne was visibly shaken. Denny took a bottle of rum from a cupboard and poured a healthy shot into a small glass. "Here, this should help you calm down."

Lynne was never a big drinker; however, she emptied the glass in one gulp.

Everyone quieted down and contemplated the situation when Walt said, "The question is; was this designed to be a random robbery, or does someone know that Captain Meyers is aboard?"

The next day Walter Ulrich, Brock McGowen, Dennis Smith and Captain Lynn Meyers became rich.

Chapter Eleven

The Eastern sky brightened with the first radiance of day-light. The men had decided to take turns on watch in case the intruders returned. Brock was first, Denny took the next watch and now Walt was taking his turn. From a fold-ing wooden chair on the stern deck, he watched the dark-ness weaken. The time between night and day is the time a boat's running lights are hardest to see. Walt did not notice until it was fully light and the top rim of the sun started peeking over the horizon, that the *Searcher* was no longer in sight. He could make out the small, white outline of some type of pleasure craft here and there on the perimeter of his sight, but nothing resembling the large Black ship.

Brock came out on deck holding two mugs of coffee and handed one to Walt.

"Thanks," Walt said. He gestured to the south, "She's gone."

At first, a look of surprise came over Brock's face. This was quickly replaced by a cagy smile. "Who's gone, the boat or the girl?"

"Both," Walt answered solemnly.

Brock looked even more surprised and asked, "Just what kind of exercise did you get last night?" A slight grin appeared on Walt's face. "A gentleman never tells ... or asks."

Brock's grin grew even larger. "You are a lucky dog," he said with envy. "How does a guy go from sitting down to dinner with a stranger to never telling in such a short time?"

Walt shrugged. "I met her on my way to the wash room. I guess it's chemistry or something."

Shaking his head, Brock mumbled, "Lucky dog."

Walt rose from the chair and stretched. Changing the subject, he asked, "What do you think about that Spaniard fellow?"

"I like the guy. He's adventurous, rich, fun loving. Hell, the more I think of it, I might want to marry him. Seriously, he seems like the kind of character I could become good friends with. Why, do you sense something different?"

"It's nothing I can put my finger on. Just a gut feeling I guess."

"It is strange he'd just up and leave like that," Brock said.

"The whole thing is strange Brock. We have a stowaway on board the boat. She shows us a treasure map. A fantastic black sailing vessel shows up with a swashbuckling Captain. Someone tries to sneak aboard our boat while we're gone ... too many coincidences. Anyway, until we find answers, we will just have to stay on our toes. Meanwhile, we'll make one dive today and then get Hollis out here with some fresh tanks."

"Yea we're going to hit it big today; the big find, treasure beyond belief. You know, the mother lode, the holy grail of treasure hunting. Oh yea, we're going to hit it big today."

That is exactly what happened.

There was only enough air left in the tanks for one more dive, but that was enough. Walt and Brock found twenty-eight mounds on the seabed of the grid they were searching. On inspection, they discovered these to have been crates. Most of the wood was gone, but the contents were intact. When extracted from the seabed, these mounds were found to be rectangular blocks. The blocks measured three feet in length by two feet wide and two feet in depth. Almost three hundred years of lying at the bottom of the sea had fused the contents to the outer shell of sea life. When Walt and Brock scraped the sea life away with their dive knives, silver appeared. They examined each mound and every one contained the same thing. The crew of the *Hunkered Down* had discovered twenty-eight crates of silver bars.

After the divers surfaced and told of the find in animated tones and gestures, work was hastily begun to bring the treasure to the surface. A sling was fashioned from heavy, three quarter inch rope. Walt and Brock would work the sling under and around one of the blocks and guide it to the surface. Using a small block and tackle, Denny would hoist the block to the boat. By the time the air in the tanks was gone, they managed to bring five blocks of silver to the stern deck of the *Hunkered Down*.

They spent the remainder of the afternoon chipping the shell of sea life away and removing the bars of silver. The bars themselves were sixteen inches in length by five inches wide and three inches thick. The ingots had turned black due to oxidation, but silver never deteriorates. Each one would be the same weight today as the day they were forged. By early evening, the crew had managed to remove every bar from one block. The block had contained fifty-six silver ingots.

Long after dark that night, the passengers aboard the *Hunkered Down* celebrated. Empty bottles of beer and a few of the silver bars crowded the galley table at which they sat. There was talk of how much was down there and of how they would go about splitting it up. Much attention was given to the subject of how each person would spend his or her share. Walt engaged in the conversation from time to time, but something was eating at him. He could not put his finger on it, but something just did not feel right.

His eyes were fixed on a bar of silver, which he held in his hands when he said, "I think we should have help."

The room fell quiet and all heads turned toward Walt. After a brief pause, Denny asked in an even tone, "Oh yea, why is that Walt?"

"I'm not sure; it's not any one thing. More like a lot of

little things ... " His voice trailed off.

Denny glanced at Brock, who after a few seconds, shrugged and took a deep swallow of beer.

Lynn, who sat next to Denny, asked a question in a way that sounded as though she already knew the answer, "You think we're in danger don't you?"

Walt set the silver bar down on the table. Counting on his fingers he said, "Someone is after the map, I've seen them on your boat. This Spaniard character shows up and by coincidence someone tries to sneak onto our boat in the middle of the night." He let out a sigh and continued, "Look, we're sitting on a treasure worth who knows how many million dollars. Unscrupulous men have already killed for it. They won't hesitate to kill again. All I'm saying is, if we do this right we'll have the rest of our lives to celebrate."

In a somber voice, Denny asked, "So what's your plan?"

"We'll keep the silver we brought up so far. There are five blocks so we'll split it up five ways. Each of us gets one block of silver and one for the little girl. After that we give the little girl fifty percent and we'll split the other fifty percent five ways between the four of us and one other partner."

"Who did you have in mind?" Brock asked. "Not Hollis I hope. I mean he's a good guy and all, but he's not exactly a superhero."

"Hollis is a darn good guy," Denny announced.

Walt said, "He is a hell of a guy I agree, but no, we need the one man who we can all trust. A man with the means, the knowhow, and the backbone to come here and take control of the situation. We need a man who gets things done."

"Art," Brock and Denny said together.

Leaning in closer to Denny, Lynn asked, "Who's Art?"

"He is without doubt, a man who gets things done."

Brock added, "Let's see, charismatic, ex-marine, successful business man and, oh yea, a mouth like a sailor."

"I agree with Walt. We could use some help," Lynn said. "But can we really trust him?"

Denny replied, "Brock and I don't know Art that well, although I wish I did know him better. Walt is good friends with Art. Why don't you tell her the story of meeting him, Walt?"

Walt leaned back in his chair and stared at the ceiling for a few seconds. Bringing his gaze back to his friends, he began to tell the story. "I was working weekends at the time as a guide for a white water rafting company in West Virginia. We were taking a large group of college students on a trip down the New River Gorge. There were six guides and about thirty-five or forty students on the trip. West Virginia has some of the top white water rapids east of the Mississippi. Carving through the rock of the gorge, the river created steep canyons. This area is also popular with rock climbers. I was guiding the lead raft and we had just rounded a bend when one of the students noticed two climbers high up on the sheer face of the cliff. We could tell in an instant that they were in trouble because the climbers were hanging upside down and swaying back and forth. We stopped at the base of the cliff, but there was little we could do other than radio home base for help. That's when Art showed up. His adventure company was just getting off the ground at the time and he was leading a small kayak excursion down the gorge. At once Art sized up the situation and took control.

To make a long story short, even though he had very limited climbing experience, Art climbed that rock himself and brought the two climbers down. A helicopter came in and evacuated them. The rest of us spent the night camped along the river and that's when I got to know Art. He's one of those people who can change the atmosphere of a room just by walking in. Art is a man of honor whose word is as good as gold. The thing that impressed me the most though, was the fact that he never mentioned the rescue. We sat around the campfire that night and every time one of the students or other guides brought it up, Art just brushed it off. He talked about doing the coolest things like exploring South America and the South Pacific."

"He sounds like a dreamer," Lynn said.

"That's what one of the students said that night at the camp fire. Art's reply was something I'll remember for the rest of my life. I can still see that scene as if it was yesterday. Deep in the West Virginia Mountains, it gets dark at night and I mean real dark, the kind of blackness not many people ever experience. I can still see Art through the blue smoke of the fire, illuminated by the glow of the flames. He said, 'We all hear the sayings and the little clichés – make the most of each day – live life to the fullest and a half a dozen more. But, how many of us ever do, and why not?'

Art goes after life and creates what he wants, not many people do that."

Brock said, "Maybe we can now that we're going to have money."

"Right," Denny agreed. "I'm with Walt. Let's bring Art in on this. That is if he'll come."

"He'll come," Walt said with confidence. "He'll come because of the pact. Walt took a drink. He looked at each person and then said, "This is the part I never told anyone, not even you guys."

His audience listened with greater intensity now. Anticipation hung thick in the air as Walt continued, "That night Art and I stayed up talking long after everyone else turned in. We became good friends in a very short time. After that, we started to take a few kayaking trips together every year and one night sitting at another fire at another camp we made a pact. The pact went like this; if either of us ever finds ourselves in trouble anywhere in the world, all we would have to do is call and the other will come."

Brock said, "Sort of like a French Foreign Legion thing."

"I guess. All I know is that I took it seriously and I know Art did too."

Denny spoke up, "Art's also the man who got us hooked up with Hollis, our go-to guy for supplies. When I talked to Hollis on the radio, he said he couldn't make it out here with the supplies and fresh tanks until about one o'clock tomorrow afternoon. Why don't I go back with Hollis to

Key West and file our claim? I'll put the ingots in storage somewhere and be back out here in a day or two."

"Sounds like a plan," Brock said before emptying his bottle of beer. The others nodded in agreement. Brock lifted another beer from the cooler and twisted the cap off. He began singing, "What will you do with a drunken sailor, what will you do with a drunken sailor?"

Walt and Denny exchanged embarrassed glances. Suddenly Lynn surprised everyone by raising her bottle in toast and singing out, loud and clear, "What will you do with a drunken sailor early in the morning."

Good-hearted laughter broke out from everyone on the boat and then they all sang another verse together, "Found him in the hold with the Captains daughter, found him in the hold with the Captains daughter, found him in the hold with the Captains daughter, early in the morning."

Well after midnight the group stayed up, drinking, singing and talking.

Chapter Twelve

By 2:30 the next afternoon, all the fresh supplies had been loaded aboard the *Hunkered Down* and Hollis and Denny were on their way back to Key West. Walt and Brock decided not to dive today. They wanted to wait until Denny filed the claim before bringing any more valuables to the surface. Instead, they would spend the afternoon relaxing and enjoying the bright sunshine. The men loaded their snorkel gear into their Prijon Seayak kayaks and paddled to Summers Cay, which was about two miles from where the *Hunkered Down* lay at anchor.

Lynn stayed aboard the boat, promising to prepare another tasty dinner if the men brought back a few speared fish. The boat was in sight of the island. In the case of any unexpected visitors, Walt and Brock could paddle back in a short time.

Beaching the kayaks on the small white sand beach, Walt and Brock swam in the gin clear shallows around the Atoll. Like many of the small islands in the Keys, Summers Cay lacked the size for development. The pristine island remained relatively untouched.

Later they spent a few hours lounging and napping on the beach, enjoying the picture-perfect day. Neither man spoke a great deal. Walt thought about Maria. Would he ever see her again? The life he wanted was so close it tantalized him. He tried not to think about the treasure, but it was no use. He knew the treasure lay only a few miles away at the bottom of the ocean, and there would be a tremendous amount of work involved in bringing it to the surface. After they recovered it, they would have to arrange to sell the treasure. Add to that the events surrounding Captain Meyers and the map, and the sum became a feeling of unease. Walt was reminded of a line from a song; send Lawyers, guns and money. We could use all three, he thought.

In the late afternoon, Walt and Brock donned their snorkel gear. They both wore Aquaflex swim fins and Alpha 4 facemasks. The men grabbed their spear guns and swam out to the deeper water on the opposite side of the island for some spearfishing.

They saw Ribbon Parrotfish and Spotted Eagle Rays. Each diver speared several Groupers and Wrasses. Fish that would make fine table fare. Walt felt like a whale as he blew the water from his snorkel to clear it. Having just surfaced, he kept his head under water and his eyes focused on a small fish close to the bottom. Feeling a tap on his shoulder, Walt was surprised to find Brock next to him. Lifting his head, he heard Brock say, "Don't look now, but I think we have company."

When Walt looked toward the island, he saw a black

speedboat beached alongside the kayaks. He immediately realized that this was one of the same black speedboats from the *Searcher.* Walt watched in disbelief as two men went to work destroying the kayaks with axes. Even at this distance, Walt recognized one of the men. He looked on as the enormous man with the square face and long hair chopped his kayak to pieces. This same man had driven the speedboat when the invitation for dinner had been made.

"Hey!" Brock yelled, waving his arms.

"Knock it off," Walt said to his friend, pulling his arm down. "I don't think we want them to see us."

Walt reacted too late. The men on the beach saw them. One man climbed into the speedboat and fired up the engine. The huge man untied the bowline and jumped in. The sleek black boat sped straight toward the men in the water.

Brock laughed and said, "OK there's two of them and two of us, I'll let you have the big guy."

"I don't think fighting is what they have in mind," Walt said, watching the big man raise a rifle to his shoulder. Despite the casual tone, Walt knew the seriousness of the situation. The uneasiness he had been feeling since the previous night had been well founded. Walt knew these men wanted the treasure. It was highly likely they had killed before and they would kill again.

As if to validate what he was thinking, the rifle cracked and a bullet zinged past Walt's head.

Brock asked, "Do you have a plan?"

"I'm not going down without a fight, that's for certain."

"How long can you hold your breath?"

"Raise your hands in surrender and be ready to act." Walt backpedaled until he was behind and slightly to Brock's right.

As the speedboat approached, it slowed and came up alongside the swimmers. With the engine idling, the big man kept the rifle trained on the two men treading water. Walt placed his left hand on Brock's shoulder. The move was sudden. With a powerful kick of his fins, Walt exploded two feet out of the water. His moves were deliberate but swift. With his right hand, he lifted the spear gun. Pointing it at the center of the big man's chest, he pulled the trigger.

The magnum spear gun drove the razor tipped shaft completely through the man's chest cavity, piercing his heart and one lung and protruding three inches from his back. The big man fired a wild shot into the air as the spear hit. He stumbled sideways into the man at the controls.

Brock was quick to catch on. Grabbing the side of the boat for leverage, he shot his spear at the back of the second man. The spear sailed high however, and glanced off the man's head opening a large gash. The combination of the big man stumbling onto him and the spear hitting his head caused the operator's hand to push the throttle forward to its stop. The bow of the speedboat leaped out of the water and the stern fish tailed. Brock tried to get clear of the wildly churning prop, but he was not fast enough. He felt a bump on his hand.

The boat tore off out of control until the operator regained command over a hundred yards away. Relief washed over Walt when he saw the boat was not circling back, but heading away. "Let's get to land," said Walt in a hurried voice.

That was when Brock lifted his hand from the water and stared in disbelief. Blood covered his left hand and his pinky and ring finger were gone.

Aboard the *Firelight*, the first mate finished tagging and releasing the White Marlin. Billy Boyd had guided many anglers in his ten years in the sport fishing industry, but this charter was without a doubt the best. In all his twenty-eight years, Billy had never met anyone with a lust for life such as this man. He was one of those larger than life characters, Billy thought as he congratulated the man with a wide grin and shook his hand.

The man on the other end of the handshake was not built physically large. Peaking at five-foot nine, he was half a foot shorter than Billy. His high and tight Marine hair cut gave him a rough and rugged look. The man had broad shoulders and a small waist giving his upper body the appearance of an upside-down triangle. His chest seemed massive, his midsection sculpted and his legs well defined. With arms that were not huge, but very well defined, he reminded Billy of the fish they were catching. The man projected nerve endings, sinewy tendons, and muscle. He was a one-hundred-and-eighty-pound ball of energy.

Standing barefoot wearing no more than a pair of cargo shorts, a watch and Costa Del Ray sunglasses, Art Kendall shook the first mate's hand with vigor. With his free hand, he gave him a firm pat on the shoulder. "Goddamned good job Billy, let's get another one and win this son of a bitch!"

They were fishing in the White Marlin Open. Over three hundred boats competing for millions of dollars in prize money made it the largest White Marlin Tournament in the world.

"OK let's do it," replied Billy, still grinning. Even though landing three Marlin in one day was a lofty goal, the intensity in the blue eyes of this client made Billy believe they could achieve that goal.

The Captain believed also, for he called down from his perch on the flying bridge high above the deck of the thirty-five foot Carolina Classic sport fishing boat, "Rig 'em up Billy. Get those lines back in the water. I'll swing her around and we'll make another pass over the lip, that's where the fish are staging," referring to the edge of the Baltimore Canyon, where the floor of the ocean drops off into extremely deep water.

While the Captain maneuvered the craft onto its new course and Billy the first mate went about rigging the rods, Art Kendall opened a cooler and took two bottles of water out. "That's two for me, now it's your turn, Barb," Art said.

"I'll bet you mine will be bigger."

"What do you want to bet, a dollar maybe?"

Barb laughed and asked, "You don't have too much confidence, do you?"

Striding across the deck as if he was born on the ocean, Art handed a bottle of water to his wife. "Hell, I have plenty of confidence."

"Well a dollar isn't a very risky wager."

"No, but the twenty-six thousand dollars I have on the line is."

Barb wore shorts, a tank top, sunglasses and a blue baseball cap with a Kendall Outdoors logo on the front. She raised the bill of the cap a bit and slid her sunglasses down onto the bridge of her nose so that Art could see her eyes. "You bet twenty-six thousand dollars on a fishing tournament?"

"Jesus H. Christ no. I bet twenty-five thousand on the tournament on the side. The other thousand was for entrance fees."

"With that kind of money involved, I think you'd better do all the fishing," Barb said, pushing her sunglasses back over her eyes.

"Like Hell I will. This is where my confidence comes in. I know for a fact that I have the best fisherwoman in the world for a wife," Art said with a broad smile.

"You're crazy."

Art began to laugh and before she could help it, Barb burst out into a long, hearty laugh. The couple laughed until they could not breathe.

Ecstasy or Crack, I wonder which one they are on, the Captain thought while running the boat from high above the deck.

What a great guy, Billy thought as he went about his duties. He could not wait to tell his girl and all his friends about the awesome client he had met.

Half an hour after the *Firelight* had started trolling over the edge of the canyon again, the third White Marlin of the day was hooked. While Billy brought in the other lines to ensure they would not become tangled, Art helped Barb settle into the fighting chair.

The epic battle between woman and fish was ten minutes old when Art heard a faint buzzing sound. He turned from the back of the fighting chair where he had been overseeing the action. The sound was barely audible but he heard the buzzing once more. Art walked over to where a small blue travel bag lay open on the deck beside the cabin door. Reaching inside, he took out a satellite phone and pulled out the antenna. Placing the phone to his ear, he pushed the talk button and said, "Art."

The high-pitched voice on the other end came back, "Hello Art, this is Hollis."

"Hollis, you little son of a bitch," Art said smiling, "how the hell are ya?" Art was not worried about offending Hollis. He knew a smile could be felt over the phone — even if it was bounced off a satellite.

"Oh, I guess I'm not too bad," Hollis said in his agonizingly slow manner. "Art, can you call me back on a land line?"

"That's a negative friend. I'm forty-five miles or so off the coast of Ocean City, Maryland."

Art glanced at Barb, who strained to control the rod and the eighty pounds of dynamite known as a White Marlin.

A few seconds passed before Hollis spoke once again, "Art can you come down to Florida?"

"Ho-lee-Hell Hollis, we're in the middle of the biggest goddamned White Marlin tournament in the world. We're right in the thick of things with a real shot at winning, and you want me to pick up and come to Florida?"

"That's what Walter Ulrich, Denny Smith and Brock McGowen wanted me to ask you," Hollis replied in a mousy voice.

"Walt. Walt's down there?"

"Yep. He's down here with two of his friends."

"Did he say anything else?"

"He said he needs you to come right away. Said you'd understand."

Art covered the mouthpiece of the phone with his hand and said, "Jesus H Christ." Now it was his turn to put a pause in the conversation. He understood all right. The pact, it had to be the pact. Only one thing would cause Walt to say those words, he was in trouble. "Where are they?"

"If you meet me, I can take you to them."

"That can be arranged." Art's tone was business like. "I can catch a flight by late afternoon or early evening. I have all of your numbers so I'll call you after the plane is chartered when I know my arrival time."

"OK, I'll tell Walter you're coming."

"Good enough," Art said, and pushed the off button on his phone. "Christ almighty," he muttered under his breath.

Art took a small brown leather address book from the travel bag. He then removed a business card from a pocket of the address book and made a call to a pilot who advertised flights to and from Ocean City Maryland. Next, he called his corporate headquarters in Ashville North Carolina. When he finished, Art placed the address book back inside the travel bag.

Walking up behind Barb, Art noticed her ponytail, which was protruding through the back of her cap swaying back and forth, as she fought the Marlin. He placed his hands on her tanned, bare shoulders and said, "Looks like you almost have this fish worn out," He said as he gently massaged her tense muscles.

"I don't know, she's still got a ton of fight left." Barb spoke in a strained voice as she cranked the handle of the large salt-water reel.

Leaning down so that his mouth was next to Barb's ear, Art said in a low tone, "I've never told this to anyone before, but watching you fish turns me on."

Barb blurted out a laugh and scolded, "Will you leave me alone so I can concentrate!"

Art laughed along with her and stood up straight, keeping his hands on her shoulders. Almost as an afterthought he asked, "What would you think of a little trip to Florida?"

"When?"

An expansive smile appeared on Art's face as he replied, "As soon as you land this big sonofabitch."

Chapter Thirteen

Blood poured from what remained of Brock's severed fingers. As the men trod water, Walt removed the rubber sling from the spear gun and fashioned a tourniquet around Brock's arm. This slowed the bleeding a great deal, but some blood still seeped from the wounds.

While they had been skirmishing with the men in the speed boat, Walt and Brock had drifted to the North West. They would now have to swim directly into the current to reach the island. The men dropped the fish they had speared, which had been fastened to their swim trunks and began to swim. Walt had Brock lie on his back and kick. He slipped his left arm under Brock's arm and around his chest, lifeguard style. The distance of half a mile, combined with the current made it a tough go. Walt was a strong swimmer however and they covered over two thirds of the distance in less than fifteen minutes. With seventy yards to go, Walt felt exhausted, but he never let up. He swam hard with powerful strokes, eating up the distance between them and land.

That is when Brock noticed the first sharks. "Trouble Walt. We have two small sharks following."

Walt did not answer, but swam even harder. The four-foot Black Tip sharks were following thirty yards behind in Walt and Brock's wake. Through the crystal-clear water, Brock could see by their movements and the way they positioned their fins, the sharks were agitated. The sharks were in-shore hunters and the blood in the water and the swimming and kicking motions of the men drew them in close. The men transmitted signals of prey.

When they were still forty yards from the beach, Brock said with urgency to his tone, "We're not going to make it! They're right on top of me." The sharks were becoming more and more brazen, weaving back and forth just behind Brock's kicking fins.

Walt continued to swim, while reaching down to unclip the spear gun from his belt. Handing the spear gun to Brock, he said, "Here, it's disabled but you might be able to use it to fend them off." He continued to swim for the beach drawing on every ounce of strength he had.

The small, fast sharks darted toward Brock's legs several times, then away again. Twice Brock used the spear gun to prod one of the Black Tips away when it came too close. One shark was shy and hung back, but the other was becoming more belligerent, continuing to make runs at Brock's feet and legs. Each time the shark became bolder.

The men were twenty yards from the beach when Brock was jerked from Walt's grip. A third shark, which had gone unseen, had come directly up from the bottom and clutched

Brock's foot, ripping him from Walt's arm and pulling him under. Biting into Brock's heel, to the bone, the shark found little meat. The four-foot Black Tip released its grip before clamping it's jaws down once again, this time lower on Brock's foot. This time it found softer flesh and with a shake of its head, the animal bit off Brock's little toe and a part of his foot.

Brock's head broke the surface with a guttural scream that started under water.

Walt was by his side in an instant. "You swim for it and I'll try to keep them off you."

Brock did not reply. He stared wide eyed at his mangled foot through the crystal clear water.

Walt took a second to glance at the foot. What he saw was awful. At least one toe and about one third of the foot was gone. Bits of bone and strands of flesh dangled and clung to the foot by a thread. A red cloud of blood was spreading fast in the water. Walt knew his friend was in deep trouble. He lost a lot of blood already and would soon go into shock. They had to swim a mere twenty yards to the beach. Land seemed so close, but it wasn't. Land was a world away and Walt and Brock were not even in that world. They were in the shark's world.

The thought of leaving his friend never entered Walt's mind. He would rather be devoured by sharks than leave Brock to die. Placing his hands on Brock's shoulders, Walt shook hard and said angrily, "Come on buddy, we're almost there." Walt then spun Brock to face the beach and encouraged him, "Swim hard! You can make it, let's go."

A shark brushed Walt's leg, but did not bite.

Brock still seemed dazed, but he lowered his head and began swimming.

Walt pulled his dive knife from its sheath strapped to his leg and followed close behind. He had only taken four strokes when he saw a shark streak in from the left. Smaller in length, this one was just over three feet, but very fast. An instant later, the shark bit down on Brock's left forearm. Walt struck like lightening. He plunged his knife into the shark's gray-skinned head. The response was immediate. The shark released its grip, turned and swam erratically away with the knife protruding from its head. Walt took Brock's knife out of the sheath strapped to his leg, gave him a shove, and yelled, "Go!"

At last, the men swam into shallow water. Just behind Brock, Walt let his feet come under him. He stood in chest deep water and took a step. As he did his right leg was yanked backwards. Spinning around, Walt saw that a shark had a hold of his swim fin. The animal's strength was tremendous. Walt was helpless as the four-foot shark began to drag him to deeper water. All at once, the shark gave a vicious shake of its head and tore half of the fin away, freeing Walt.

The Black Tip mouthed the piece of fin for a moment before dropping it and in a nonchalant fashion swam away. This body language had a calming effect on the other Black Tips, whose numbers had increased to eight. The sharks maintained their rigid posture but they backed off and no longer appeared to be interested in the men.

Walt breathed a sigh of relief as he realized they would make the last few yards to land. Turning to the direction of Brock, Walt froze at the sight of the dark shape heading straight for his friend's good leg. The men swimming, the blood, and the agitated action of the other sharks worked to attract another predator. This one was not a small Black Tip. This was a big, bulky, seven-foot Bull shark.

Walt had no time to think. He dove, stretching out completely. Man and shark came together only one foot from Brock's leg. Walt stabbed the knife into the big shark's eye, which had just begun to roll closed. The seven-inch blade sank in to the hilt. Thrashing and rolling, the shark went berserk. The water frothed as the Bull shark snapped its jaws and undulated. Walt pushed Brock out of the way and then helped him up. The two men staggered to the beach.

The knife dislodged from its eye as the Bull Shark swam for deep water. A three-foot Black Tip crossed lazily in front of the Bull. The big Bull bit right through the Black Tip, cutting the smaller shark in half and disappeared in a flash of clouded pink water.

Hollis and Denny moored the boat at Key West Bight Marina. Hollis had backed his nineteen eighty-eight Chevrolet pickup truck right up to the dock. After he had made the call to Art, Hollis helped Denny begin to unload the bars of silver from the boat onto the bed of the truck.

After spending the last several days on a boat on the

ocean, Denny's legs felt like rubber, the land seemed to slant this way and that. By the time the truck was loaded, he found his land legs once more. With the last bar loaded, the truck sagged on its springs from the weight. Denny had just slammed the tailgate closed when he heard a click and felt an object press against the back of his head.

A voice came from behind, "Turn around slowly, señor."

Turning to face the man, he saw a semi-automatic pistol aimed at his head. Hollis came around the side of his truck. A man carrying a small-bore shotgun followed him. Denny recognized the man as the crewmember with the thin mustache from the *Searcher*.

The man said with a thin smile, "Sorry to double your work. We were hoping to get here before you unloaded your cargo, but you may now remove it from the truck and load it onto our boat."

Walt retrieved the first aid kit from the wreckage of his kayak and went to work on Brock. The foot injury looked the most serious so that is where he began. Brock's left heel was ravaged. His little toe and a section of his foot shaped in a semi-circle were missing. Walt cleaned the wound and bandaged the entire foot. Next, he dragged one of the kayaks over and placed Brock's leg on top of it. This raised the wound and slowed the bleeding.

Concentrating on Brock's forearm next, Walt cleaned and bandaged those wounds. Even though the shark had barely closed its jaws before Walt's knife penetrated its head, the teeth left a set of deep bite wounds. The wounds did not bleed a great deal due to the tourniquet, applied earlier to slow the bleeding from Brock's fingers. Before going to work on the fingers, Walt released the tourniquet to allow circulation return to the arm and hand. Without delay, blood began to pour from the severed fingers. After a short time, Walt reapplied the tourniquet. Finally, he cleaned and bandaged the stumps of Brock's pinky and ring fingers. With this done, he removed the tourniquet for good.

For the first time since making the beach, Walt spoke, "Now that was something you don't see every day. How are you doing?"

"I'm OK," Brock replied with a weak smile. "Except for the part of knowing I'm going to die, I'm having a great time. This is a terrific vacation."

"I hate to disappoint you pal, but you're a long way from dead."

"Not too many people can say they were attacked by sharks. If I do live, the women will love me."

Walt laughed, but his light tone disguised his deep concern. Brock was in serious condition. He had lost a great deal of blood and would need immediate medical attention. Large slashes and holes rendered the Kayaks useless.

Rubbing his hand over his eyes, Walt took a moment to think things through. At last, he said, "I'm going for help. I'll have to leave you here, but I won't be gone for long."

"Where are you going to find help?"

"The *Hunkered Down.*"

"How are you going to get there?"

"I'll have to swim."

"Ha! Ha!" Brock laughed. "The boat is over two miles away, you'll never make it."

"I'll make it. You try and relax until I get back." Walt was not looking forward to a two-mile swim in the open ocean so close to where a shark attack occurred. He had no choice, his friend needed help and swimming was the only option. The *Hunkered Down* lay at anchor on the opposite side of the island. Walt thought that maybe the sharks would not notice him. Even if they did, they might not bother with him.

Walt waded out into the shallow water and washed the blood off his hands and arms. When he finished, he set out for the far side of the island. Half way across Walt froze in his tracks. The black ship *Searcher* floated alongside the *Hunkered Down.* He was too late. The Spaniard was a pirate. *Searcher* was a pirate ship. Walt felt certain the pirates would have boarded the *Hunkered Down* by now. Captain Meyers could be in tremendous danger, but he could do nothing now. Perhaps after dark he could try a rescue. Walt's mind was racing as he hurried back to the beach.

He arrived to find Brock singing, "What will you do with a drunken sailor?"

Walt squatted down beside Brock, "That idea's shot. The Spaniard's ship is alongside the *Hunkered Down.*"

Grimacing, Brock said, "This is a good time for plan B."

"Don't worry; we'll come up with something," Walt replied, noticing a white boat off in the distance. The boat was heading in their direction from the north. This area provided good sport fishing and other recreational activities. It was not uncommon to spot various small craft in the vicinity.

Walt moved fast. He took a red life jacket from the kayak and tied it to the end of one of the paddles. Holding the paddle straight over his head, he began to wave the life jacket back and forth. The boat continued to approach and Walt could now see that it was a sport yacht. As the yacht came on, Walt dropped the paddle and waved his arms over his head, "Hey, over here!"

The boat slowed and entered the shallows. Relief flooded over Walt as he recognized the man speaking into a two-way radio on the deck of the yacht. He was the same man Walt had met on the dock at Key West, the big Australian man from New Zealand.

"Mr. Haggarty, we need assistance," Walt called.

Billy Haggerty set the radio mike down and asked in his thick accent, "Walter, is that you?"

"Yes, it's Walter Ulrich. We've had a shark attack here; can you help us?"

"Of course, mate, hold on."

Fifty yards from where Brock lay, the water was deep enough so the yacht could tie off directly to one of the shrubs on the island. This way, the men could get Brock aboard without going into the water. Haggarty's mate Jonna helped Walt lift Brock into the boat. The men laid Brock on the deck and made him as comfortable as possible. Not until this was finished, did Walt explain what had happened. He told the story of the pirates and the shark attack, leaving out the discovery of the shipwreck. The men believed it would be best to get moving as soon as possible, in case the pirates decided to return. Haggarty said he would call the Coast Guard as soon as they were under way. Jonna fired up the engine and pushed the throttle forward. As soon as the bow came on plane, he swung the boat around the tip of the island.

Walt ran up behind the man and put a hand on his shoulder. The *Hunkered Down* and the *Searcher* were coming in to sight as Walt said, "That's a bad idea. This course will take us right past The Spaniard."

"Not right past mate," Walt heard Haggerty's voice behind him. Turning, He found Haggerty holding a nine-millimeter semi- automatic pistol pointed at his chest. With a sinister grin, Haggerty continued, "Not right past The Spaniard, right to him."

Walt had a moment of clarity. The moment started in a haze, but then blew through the fog like a runaway train. The little Cuban girl had told Lynn that one of the men who took her father away was dark with long hair and funny drawings on his face, when he looked at Jonna that statement came barreling back to him. He had wondered before but the connection had slipped his mind. Now it came back with a bang. Walt stared in disbelief at the dark man with long, black curls and the Maori tribal tattoos on his face. Haggarty and The Spaniard were working together. While The Spaniard entertained Walt and his friends, Haggarty and his mate tried to sneak aboard the *Hunkered Down* and steal the treasure map.

Chapter Fourteen

Walt stood on the deck of the *Searcher* with his hands on his hips. He found himself surrounded by two crewmembers with automatic rifles, Haggarty, and the Maori. Brock lay at his feet with a hand covering his eyes. He was in obvious pain.

Glancing around, Walt noticed two rubber fenders, placed between *Hunkered Down*, and *Searcher*, which bound the boats together. The fenders were to prevent damage from the two boats coming together. Rope lines secured the *Hunkered Down* to *Searcher* and a rope ladder led from the starboard gunwale of *Searcher* to the deck of the *Hunkered Down*. Haggerty's yacht was tied to the stern rail of *Searcher*. The two black speedboats were along the port side. A female crewmember was cleaning blood from one of the boats. A man in the other boat was busy preparing to leave. Lying across the rear seat of the boat Walt saw a large object wrapped in canvas.

The Spaniard emerged from the bridge and stood face to face with Walt, "Walt, good to see you."

"I wish I could say the same."

The Spaniard smiled and said, "Now, Now, if anyone should be upset it is I." Pointing at the speedboat he continued, "You killed one of my crew and my friend. He was a good man."

Walt had not known the outcome of the spear he had shot through the big man's chest until now. Guilt flooded over him. He realized that the object wrapped in canvas was the body of a man he had killed. The feeling of guilt did not last very long. "I'm sorry for him, but it was kill or be killed. He shot at me first."

"No, that was a misunderstanding. I can assure you, the shot he fired was meant to be a warning. His orders were to bring you here, alive and well." The Spaniard paused before asking, "What do you think of me? I am not a cold-blooded murderer."

"Good. We need to get Brock some medical attention. Since you're such a great guy," Walt added with heavy sarcasm, "I'm sure you'll be happy to help."

Haggarty stepped forward and pointed at Brock, "He's no use to us mate. I say we throw this piece of meat over the side. The sharks got a good start on him, let them finish the job."

The crack sounded like a fat man doing a belly flop in a shallow swimming pool. Walt's fist connected squarely with Haggarty's bulbous nose. The massive man swayed on his feet for a long second before staggering backward and falling on his side.

The Maori pounced like a cat. Before Walt could react,

the man wrapped one arm around his neck and the other behind his head in a deadly chokehold.

The Spaniard stepped forward. "Release him," he ordered. When the Maori did not yield, The Spaniard repeated, "Release him, now!"

With ill-disguised resentment, the Maori complied, releasing his grip and stepping away.

Haggarty raised himself to a sitting position. He pulled a white handkerchief from his pocket and held it to his bleeding nose. "You will pay dearly for this," he hissed.

Walt's temper flared, "You'd better bring your Maori buddy along, because I'll kick your ass all over this ocean."

"That is enough!" the Spaniard shouted. To Haggerty, he said, "We are not going to kill anyone." He told Walt, "You've already met Dr. Qeuokas. I'll have him treat your friend."

Walt realized that even though he would love to have a go at Haggarty and the Maori, he needed a cool, clear head. His survival and the survival of the others depended on it. "Where is Captain Meyers?" he asked.

"The Captain is below. She is fine." The Spaniard sighed. "Despite the actions of my partners, I assure you I meant no harm to come to you. There will be no more fighting and above all else, no killing."

Haggarty walked to a far corner of the deck with the Maori close behind. He kept his head tilted back and the handkerchief over his nose, trying to stop the bleeding.

The Spaniard summoned Doctor Qeuokas. He told him to help Brock first, and then have a look at Haggarty's obviously broken nose. With the help of two crewmembers, the Doctor carried Brock below to be treated.

The Spaniard glanced at his watch and announced, "I believe we have time for one more dive before dark. I hope you will oblige Walter. All we want is the treasure. You will do the diving. Use your head. I have a share reserved for each of the four of you. I am a peaceful man, but if you try anything, it will not be good for your friends Brock and the Captain. Haggarty is ... what is the saying ... chomping up the bit."

"Chomping at the bit," Walt corrected.

Showing a brilliant smile, the Spaniard said, "Why must you Americans make your language so difficult? Oh well, no matter." Giving Walt a pat on the back he continued, "What do you say Walt? I believe you and I could become good friends."

Walt did not give an immediate answer.

The trouble was; he thought the same thing.

Had The Spaniard not been stealing from him, Walt could see himself becoming friends with this man.

"How did you become involved with a man like him?" Walt asked in a low voice.

"That is a long story, but the bottom line is, Haggarty loves money and I love the lifestyle money provides."

———

As Walt checked the scuba gear one last time, he asked in a whisper, "You hear anything from Denny?"

Lynn replied by shaking her head no.

Walt frowned. The Spaniard knew Denny had been aboard the *Hunkered Down*, and yet he made no mention of him.

In the soft orange glow of the evening light, the reason became apparent. Walt saw a boat approaching from the south. A crewmember tied the small, unadorned boat to the transom of *Searcher*. When he finished, another crewmember herded two men toward a rope ladder. Walt saw that the two men were Denny and Hollis.

Denny noticed Walt and raised his hands, palms up, in a hopeless expression.

With half of the sun already below the horizon, Walt winked at Denny, pulled his mask on, and slipped over the side. After the events of the day, Walt felt nervous about being in the water, especially in low light. He could not believe how dark it was below the surface. As he descended through the inky water, he warily eyed his surroundings.

Upon reaching the bottom, Walt stopped looking. Visibility was so limited; he would be unable to see a shark until it was right on top of him. His old saying, you have to die of something, came to mind and put the thoughts of shark attacks out of his head. Considering his situation, a shark attack was only one of many ways he could go. Besides, he had plenty of other problems to keep his mind occupied. He needed to stay focused.

Walt towed the sling to the closest block of ingots, but he did not begin to slip the sling underneath just yet. He had one and a half hours of air in his tank so he took his time. He needed time alone, time to think. Denny and Hollis were alive, that was a relief. Did they get in touch with Art? Help could be on the way if they did, if not, they were on their own. The Spaniard was a pirate, but he did not come across as a murderer. Haggarty, on the other hand, would not think twice about killing all five of them.

The fact that the Spaniard had sent Walt down, caused him to believe that none of the pirates were adept divers. That being the case, they would need Walt and his friends, at least until they finished bringing the treasure up. The best thing to do, he decided, would be to play along for a few days. Sometime, somehow, if rescue did not come, they would have to look for an opening and try to escape.

Walt worked the sling around the block, but waited another five minutes before heading to the surface. On a daylight dive, the surface looks bright. Shimmering silver sunlight penetrates the water. At that time of evening, all Walt saw as he rose was a very pale pink at the surface. Silently, a school of small fish crossed Walt's field of view near the surface. The silvery fish swam past and faded into the gloom. This gave Walt an idea. Thinking that every minute counted, he would try to buy some time.

Walt broke the surface twenty feet from the *Hunkered Down*. He swam rapidly to the boat and climbed the dive ladder. "We have sharks in the water."

The Spaniard, the crewman with the thin mustache, Lynn, and Jonna the Maori waited on the deck of the *Hunkered Down*. They all stared back at him. No one spoke.

"I have the sling attached, but there are a couple of big sharks roaming around down there. It's too dark for another dive, we have to wait until morning or I'll be a sitting duck."

"No, we will not wait," the Maori said. "You will dive now and guide the sling to the surface."

Walt was having a bad day. First, a man shot at him. Next, there was the shark attack. Haggarty betrayed him. The Spaniard turned out to be a pirate. He felt exhausted and now he was told to dive again in the dark. Walt had enough. His temper flared once more. Looking the Maori straight in the eye, he held up a finger and said, "There is only one way I'm going in the water again tonight."

"And what is that?"

"If you come with me." Walt made a run at the Maori and wrapped his arms around the man. His momentum carried them both over the side. They hit the water with a loud smack. A smile formed on Walt's face. His opponent was a quick, sinewy, strong man, but Walt wore fins. He was not a fighter. However, Walter Ulrich would take on any man in the water. Given the edge of wearing fins, he figured the odds to swing greatly in his favor.

Besides that, Walt was now royally ticked off.

The mustached crewmember started to draw his pistol, but sensing that Walt had the advantage, the Spaniard grabbed him by the arm. "No, let them go. I'm tired of hearing that tattooed man's big mouth."

The two men parted as they hit the water. Unhooking the harness, Walt dropped his air tank at once, letting it sink to the bottom. The Maori turned and swam for the boat, frightful of the sharks he believed would be on him any second. He did not know that sharks were the least of his worries. Walt gave his fins a few powerful kicks and came up behind the man in an instant. As the Maori tried to scramble up the side of the boat, Walt aimed a punch at his kidneys. The punch would have been devastating if thrown through the air, but the water slowed it down. Even so, his fist landed with enough force to cause the man to gasp in pain. When the Maori gasped, he breathed in a great deal of salt water. Walt did not let up. He threw a short left cross at the man's head. The punch pushed Jonna's head under water. In a flash, Walt mounted the other man's shoulders, wrapping his legs tightly around his neck. By moving his arms, Walt could stay afloat while keeping his foe under water.

This fight was over. Walt was not sure what came over him, and he did not care. He killed a man earlier with a spear gun and now, he was going to kill this man. Walt felt nothing ... no regret ... nothing. He would hold this Maori man under until he drowned.

Out of the corner of his eye, Walt noticed movement aboard the *Searcher*. On the rear deck, high above the *Hunkered Down*, Haggarty raised a pistol. He cocked the hammer and aimed at Walt. Without warning, a figure leapt out of the shadows and gave Haggarty a shove. Haggarty stumbled just as he pulled the trigger. The bullet went high and wild, not coming anywhere close to Walt.

Abruptly the Spaniard raised his hands and shouted,

"Enough!" He pointed at Haggarty and ordered, "You, stop." He pointed to Walt and demanded, "You, let him up. Now."

Walt exhaled a long breath. He knew he had no choice. Releasing his grip, he backstroked a few yards.

Jonna the Maori came up coughing and wheezing for air. Walt trod water and looked up at *Searcher*. While the Maori gathered his wits, and started to swim for the boat, Walt glanced at Haggarty. He held the gun at his side and he held his venomous stare on Walt. At the first opportunity, Walt knew the big Australian would try to kill him.

The person who came to the rescue stood beside Haggarty, clutching the rail. In the fading light, Walt made out the sleek black hair and delightful face. The gorgeous, dark eyes gazing down upon him belonged to Maria.

The Spaniard decided to wait until morning before the diving resumed. For the night, Lynn and Hollis would be kept under guard aboard the *Hunkered Down*. Walt, Denny, and Brock would sleep in cabins aboard *Searcher*. Before the armed crewmember led him to his room, Walt insisted on seeing Brock.

The doctor was with Brock when Walt looked in on him. He had just finished applying hundreds of stitches to Brock's wounds. He had administered antibiotics and strong pain medication through a drip,. Brock breathed easy in a deep sleep. Walt received an assurance from the

doctor that if infection did not set in, his friend would recover.

After checking in on Brock, the armed crewman guided
Walt to his room. A guard stood watch outside the door.
Walt entered the cabin and sat on the edge of the bed. He
felt bone tired. After a few minutes, he dragged himself to
the tiny bathroom and took a long, hot shower. Following
the shower, Walt noticed that his belongings were in the
corner of the cabin. Removing a shaving kit, he shaved and
brushed his teeth before leaving the bathroom. Not bothering to dress, Walt lay on the bed above the sheets and gathered his thoughts. He wondered if the guard posted outside
his door was armed, deciding at once that it did not matter.
The Spaniard warned him earlier that if anyone tried to
escape, everyone would pay a high price. Walt had experi-
enced enough skullduggery for one day.

He hadn't had a chance to talk to Denny. The big question was; did Hollis have enough time to call Art Kendall or
not? Until he found out whether help was on the way, he
would have to do the pirates bidding.

Walt was drifting toward sleep when he heard the latch
on the cabin door open. He remained still, keeping his eyes
closed. It is Jonna the Maori coming for revenge, Walt
speculated. Hearing light footsteps approach his bed, he lay
poised for an attack. Walt had the upper hand in the water,
but not now. He thought that maybe he could gain an edge
by surprising the man. He needed an edge, for he could tell
the Maori knew his way around hand-to-hand combat.

Walt felt the presence of someone standing over him. He closed his fist and was about to strike, when he detected a light, sweet scent of perfume. Walt's eyes snapped open and there before him stood Maria.

Maria smiled and her eyes traveled over his body. It was her turn to see Walt without clothes. "I see you dressed for the occasion," she said, before leaning over and kissing him.

Chapter Fifteen

The sixty-year-old pilot fired up the engine and the propel-
ler came to life. As he completed running through his pre-
flight checklist, Art Kendall took his seat behind the pilot,
and beside his wife.

Barb looked up from her i-pad and asked, "Are we all
set?"

"All set. The pilot said we'll be taking off in a few
minutes," Art answered, checking his watch. The time was
11:55 pm. The earliest chartered flight Art could get was
midnight. He felt relieved to know they would be taking off
on time. They were flying in a four seater Cessna TTx.
With maximum cruising speed of 235 KTAS, or true air
speed, and a range of 1,270 nautical miles, the pilot assured
Art he would have them in Key West by morning.

"Do you seriously believe that Walt is in trouble?" Barb
asked.

Art reached out and took her hand. Giving her a light
squeeze, he said, "Hell if I know. I do know Walt, and he
wouldn't ask me to come to Florida unless it was damn im-

portant."

"The pact."

"Affirmative."

"How many people did you make this pact with?"

"Oh ... three, maybe four."

"Well," Barb asked, "is it three or is it four? I'm sure you keep track of something like this."

"Officially it's three, plus you makes four."

Barb smiled and laid her head back against the headrest. Today was the first time that she heard of the pact. She understood and was not upset that Art never mentioned it before. This pact was made among men, her kind of men. Art and his small group of close friends were not the type to loaf around drinking beer and watching football on Sundays. They were men of action, men of honor. While some women might consider picking up and flying through the night, just because a friend asked you to, boyish, she expected no less of her husband. To Barb, family and friends is all there is and how you take care of each other is all that matters.

She did feel nervous however, not knowing what they were getting into. "Must be great."

"What's that?" asked Art

"You're not afraid of anyone or anything, are you?"

As the props sputtered and then the engines of the plane came to life, Art's voice rose above the roar, "You don't know me as well as you thought. There's one person who scares me half to death."

"Who's that?"

"You."

Art saw the skeptical look on Barb's face so he explained, "I'm not scared of you, I'm scared of disappointing you." He checked his watch again, "Midnight, let's get this goddamned show on the road."

The plane began a slow taxi. Barb turned to the window. She could see the huge smile that had appeared on her face, in her reflection in the glass. She felt elated and tears welled up in her eyes. As the plane gained altitude and the lights of the Ocean City boardwalk came into view, Barb's smile never faded.

Walt felt exhausted, but sleep did not come.

Maria rolled onto her side to face him. "You should sleep."

He shook his head and said, "I just don't get it. I kind of like your brother. You're OK too."

"I am just OK?" she asked, playfully tickling him.

He laughed and continued, "But, you're pirates. There's no other way to put it. You and your brother are pirates. That doesn't make sense."

Maria ran her fingers through Walt's hair. "We've searched for this treasure for a long time. You found the treasure, and we found you. We will split the money and everyone will be happy. I know my brother will give the four of you a large cut."

"And he'll allow us to walk away as if nothing happened?"

"Of course, Juan has a good heart. He is not a murderer. He would never hurt anyone. Also, he likes you."

"What about Haggerty? You think he's going to let us go?"

Maria frowned and spat, "Haggerty is a pig. His tattooed friend is the devil."

Walt shook his head and sighed. "That's what's hard for me to fathom. How did people of your class get mixed up with them?"

A serious expression came over Maria's face. She said, "Juan made a mistake. For ten years, we sailed the ocean, the same as our ancestors hundreds of years ago. We took what we wanted, but we never hurt anyone. My brother always made sure to deal fairly with anyone we were involved with. Juan's exploits proved to be very profitable. We have vast holdings worth millions. We own prime estates on the best seafront properties around Europe." Maria hesitated before stating, "We knew of the sinking of the *Santa Luala* because one of our ancestors was aboard when she went down."

Walt asked, "Your ancestor was the Spanish officer who survived?"

"Yes, officer Alvereze. When he returned to Havana in 1717, he spoke of the wreck, except he gave the wrong location. The authorities launched a costly salvage operation. After spending a great deal of the King of Spain's money and finding nothing, the search was called off."

"They were searching the wrong spot." Walt said.

"Yes, the Governor of Cuba at that time was determined to remain in power, so he never reported the *Santa Luala* sinking, or the failed salvage attempt. He reported to Spain that the ship had gone missing, nothing more.

Officer Alvereze spent two years locked in prison to keep him from telling his story to the King. Eventually, he escaped. He falsified his identity and made his way back to Spain aboard another ship. There, he met and married a local woman. He changed his name once again out of fear the governor of Cuba might find out his whereabouts and fabricate a false accusation against him. The man had far-reaching connections.

Other than his wife and children, Officer Alvereze never told anyone his identity. He spent the rest of his life trying to raise money to salvage the treasure of the *Santa Luala.*"

"Let me guess, this legend has been passed down through your family from generation to generation."

"Yes, that is correct, the diary, detailing the location of the wreck along with the money each generation saved for the salvage has been handed down. Alvereze's son became a pirate as his way of raising money. He raided several English ships and amassed a great fortune. His career ended when one of his own crew killed him. You can see that piracy is in our blood."

Maria paused for a moment in reflection. Finally, she continued, "As each generation saved money and passed it on, our family eventually became quite wealthy. My brother is the first one to go out and search for the treasure. There was a large problem however; a fire destroyed the diary when Juan and I were children. We knew of one other survivor, so Juan hired an international private detective."

"Haggerty." Walt said.

"Yes. He used to be a spy or something before going into business for himself. He agreed to a price, but when he found out the map really existed, he demanded to become a partner. Only after accepting him as a partner did we learn what kind of man he really is. Our best option is to bring the treasure up and allow Haggerty to go on his way, and we will go our own way. I am certain you can see that."

"I still don't believe Haggerty will allow my friends and I to have one dime of the treasure," Walt said.

They heard the pitter-patter of rain softly falling on the decks of the boat. Maria kissed Walt on the cheek and said, "Do not worry, The Spaniard will keep Haggerty in his place." Her kisses continued down his neck as the rain fell harder.

The rain stopped just before dawn. At seven a.m., the air temperature was already in the low nineties, and humidity was high. Walt sweated buckets under his wet suit. He had left Maria an hour ago. Mixed emotions tugged at Walt. On the one hand, he wanted to believe the beautiful woman who now slept in his bunk. The Spaniard came across as a man Walt would spend time with. However, he knew Juan Chavez was a thief ... a modern-day pirate. Because Brock was laid up with his injuries, Denny would be diving with

Walt today. Checking his regulator, Walt said, "Today's going to be a scorcher; it's a good day to be diving." He hoped his calm demeanor would put his friend at ease.

Denny, who sat beside Walt on the gunwale of the boat said, "Yea, it'll be a lot cooler underwater."

The Spaniard stood behind the divers, "Do not forget the conversation we had at breakfast."

Earlier, Walt, Denny, Lynn, and Hollis had eaten a light breakfast of fruit and cereal with the Spaniard in the *Searcher's* salon. The Spaniard had explained what he expected from each of them. Walt and Denny would do the diving, while Lynn and Hollis helped with the recovery. The Spaniard and Haggarty would each take twenty five percent. The other half was theirs to keep and split any way they saw fit. The Spaniard assured everyone; no harm would come to anyone, if no one disobeyed his orders.

Walt finished his preparations and looked at Denny. His friend nodded and the two men slipped over the side and into the water.

"Be careful," Lynn said under her breath.

The moment the divers reached the bottom, Walt used his gloved finger to scratch the seafloor. He carved the letters Art in the gravel bottom and then held his pinky and thumb to the side of his head in the gesture of holding a telephone.

Denny understood and replied with a vigorous nod of his head.

A feeling of elation came over Walt. This was great news. Someone would be looking for them. Walt decided that the best thing to do would be to play along, wait it out.

Art Kendall was on the way.

———— ♦ ————

Art turned the Ford Escape onto the gravel driveway. Bringing the rental car to a stop in front of Hollis's front door, he turned off the ignition and glanced around. Hollis told Art he would meet him at the Key West International Airport. Art tried repeatedly to reach him by phone to give him their arrival time. When he got no answer, he decided to rent a car and drive to Hollis's house. Art knew Hollis and knew he kept his appointments.

"Doesn't look like he's home," said Art.

There were no vehicles in sight, Barb noted. "What does he drive?"

"The last time I saw him he had an old pickup truck. Come on let's see if he's in."

Hollis lived in a small, weather beaten, wooden clapboard house. The small amount of paint that remained on the wood was battleship grey and flaking. Art and Barb walked up the creaky steps to the wooden porch. He opened the screen door and knocked sharply on the wooden front door. After several attempts without a reply, he said, "Let's have a look around."

Hollis had several sheds and out buildings behind his house. Art and Barb found boat parts, cutting torches, engines, electrical motors, and air compressors. However, they found no sign of Hollis James.

Art inhaled a deep breath. From the Hollis household, he could see the ocean. Walter Ulrich and his friends were in some type of trouble. Of that, he felt certain. What type of trouble, and how Hollis figured in the mix of things he did not know?

Making a quick decision, he turned to Barb. "Let's go get some breakfast."

"You don't want to search for Hollis?"

"I do," Art said, "but I don't know where to start, other than to start asking around. We'll ask some questions at the diner. That'll give his neighbors some time to wake up."

Art and Barb returned to the car and left. They made plans to look for Hollis at the docks after breakfast and come by again to talk to the neighbors if they were still unable to find him.

Chapter Sixteen

Walt and Denny spent the morning bringing blocks of silver bars to the surface. At eleven o'clock, they took a break. The galley crew of *Searcher* prepared a light brunch of tuna salad. After finishing, Walt, Denny, Lynn, and Hollis lounged on the bow of the *Hunkered Down*. The small group of captives was kept under the close watch of Jonna and the crewman with the thin mustache.

After a morning of being under water, Walt relaxed and relished the time he spent drying out in the warm sunlight. His relaxation was short lived, interrupted by Hollis's slow, drawn out voice.

"We have to do something."

Walt pointed to the north. The sun shone bright over their position but one mile away, a large, dark thunderhead rolled across the horizon. Heavy rain could be seen falling and the sea was choppy underneath the clouds. The warm water and cooler air created a water witch. The funnel, which rose from the sea to the clouds, captured everyone's attention.

In a hushed tone, Walt said, "Everyone stay cool. If these pirates are going to harm us, and I'm not sure they will, it won't be until after all or most of the treasure is recovered."

Walt sensed that Haggerty would not let them live. After bringing up the treasure, and they were no longer needed, they would be killed.

"And there's a great deal of treasure still down there," Denny added.

"Right," Walt agreed, "we have at least a few more days. Art Kendall is probably on his way. Our best bet is to wait for help."

Lynn's face showed the strain of the situation. "I hope this Art Kendall fellow is a man of his word."

Walt readied a new air tank to replace the one he dropped in the fight with Jonna the Maori. He picked up his wetsuit and began to put it on. He stopped and turned his head when he heard a familiar voice. The voice belonged to Maria. Walt watched her walking across *Searcher's* deck speaking in Spanish to the Spaniard. Doctor Qeuokas and his wife followed close behind.

Walt dropped his wetsuit. Barefoot and wearing only his swim trunks, he made his way to the portable stairway that connected the *Hunkered Down* to *Searcher*. Placing a foot on the first step, he found his way blocked by the Jonna the Maori.

The Maori put his hand on Walt's chest and said, "No, go back."

"This will only take a minute."

"Go back," The Maori repeated.

Walt did not back down. He held his ground, staring the man down. After a few seconds, Walt decided to try another angle. He stepped back and called, "Señorita Chavez, good afternoon!"

Maria turned and walked to the starboard rail. "Buenos Dias Walt. How is everything going?" she asked, with a pretty smile.

Walt wondered if the Spaniard knew that his sister had left his bed no more than a few hours ago. If he did know, he did not let it show.

"I'd like to speak to you, may I come aboard?"

"Of course, Walt, you need not ask permission," Maria replied.

Walt stared at the Maori and gave him a smirk as he passed by.

The Maori eyed him with an intimidating glare. He said in a low tone, "Soon ... very soon."

Brushing the threat off, Walt continued up the stairway with a bounce in his step.

The Spaniard and his sister met Walt upon reaching the deck. Once more, he inhaled the sweet scent of her perfume. The doctor and his wife were boarding the boat used to bring Denny, Hollis, and the five blocks of silver back from Key West.

Maria greeted Walt by hugging him. She then stood on her tiptoes and gave him a light kiss on the lips. If the Spaniard did not know of the situation between Maria and Walt before, he had to know now.

"Is there a problem?" The Spaniard asked.

"No problem with the dive. I am worried about Brock. I'd like to speak to the doctor."

"Of course, be my guest," The Spaniard replied with a sweep of his arm.

Walt walked to the stern rail and called, "Doctor."

The doctor and his wife sat in the small craft, which was tied off to a cleat on the stern of *Searcher*. Doctor Qeuokas looked up and asked, "Walter, how are you?"

"I'm fine. I was wondering how Brock's doing?"

"He is gaining his strength; therefore, I do not believe the loss of blood will be a factor. The wounds appear clean. So long as infection does not set in, I am certain he will make a full recovery, besides missing a few digits and having some scars."

"That's good news," Walt said. "Are you leaving?"

Maria answered for the doctor, "Yes, we have some arrangements to make." She placed her hand on Walt's bare upper arm with a light touch. "After all, finding the treasure is only the first step. Now it must be resold."

Maria descended the portable aluminum ladder and boarded the small craft. The doctor started the engine while she took a seat beside Mrs. Qeuokas.

As the doctor maneuvered the boat away from *Searcher*, Maria looked back over her shoulder and called, "Good luck with your diving. Take care."

The doctor nudged the throttle and the boat picked up speed. Maria turned away and did not look back.

In that moment, something clicked in Walt's head. It

was as though a light switch had suddenly been turned on. Watching the boat speed away, bouncing on an occasional wave, Walt saw Maria clearly, more accurately, he saw right through her.

Maria was the type of women who could walk into your life, turn you on your head, and walk right out, without ever looking back. She was beautiful and alluring, but she had no soul. He had the feeling that Maria had used many men in her lifetime and would no doubt use many more.

Walt was no fool. He vowed not to be taken in by her false charm. This was a dangerous game and he would need all his wits if he and his friends were going to survive.

The Spaniard stepped beside Walt and in a polite tone said, "If there's nothing else, perhaps the diving could resume?"

"Yes, of course. I know you're still in a hurry to have your money."

"Our money," the Spaniard corrected. "As I told you, everyone gets a share. We can discuss this at greater length over dinner tonight, but for now ... "

"I know," Walt interjected, starting for the gangway, "back to the dive."

By sunset, every one of the blocks of silver were above the surface of the sea. Their weight would have been too much for the *Hunkered Down*, so most of the load was transferred to the *Searcher*.

At eight o'clock Walt sat down at the spacious mahogany dining room table in the salon. The delicious aromas coming from the Galley made his stomach growl in anticipation. Hollis took a seat to his left. Denny and Lynn sat across from him. Walt wore Teva sandals, shorts, and his blue Tommy Bahama aloha shirt. He had felt dead tired when he finished diving, but an invigorating hot shower had brought him back to life. Walt was famished, looking forward to a hearty meal. He also felt relieved to see that Haggarty was not present. He could do without that constant pressure during dinner.

Dinner began with Spanish Style Chickpeas and Shrimp soup. The Spaniard stood and raised his glass, "A toast. To the *Santa Luala.*"

"And to the men who went down with her," Walt added somberly.

The Spaniard bowed his head slightly and everyone joined in the toast.

The soup was an appetizer. When everyone finished, thick steaks were served. The steaks were in honor of his American guests, The Spaniard announced. While they ate, the group discussed the wreck and the treasure. The Spaniard asked most of the questions. Walt and the others supplied the answers.

They informed the Spaniard of the cobs Walt noted lying on the sea floor. The cobs became exposed when the bottom was stirred up during the recovery of the silver. A cob was the name for a coin used during the time of the Spanish treasure fleet. Everyone wondered whether the cobs would be made of gold, silver, or both, since gold and silver cobs were listed in the ship's manifest.

There were many other treasures to discuss such as

pearls, emeralds and rubies ... riches beyond belief. The atmosphere in the salon was casual. The Spaniard remained friendly and seemed genuinely interested in each of his guests. He asked about their lives and answered openly and honestly when asked about his own.

Without Haggarty or any other outside interference, the evening went well. The Spaniard, Walt thought, was a fun loving, vigorous man. Even though he was a pirate, Walt enjoyed his company.

After dinner, an armed crewman escorted Lynn and Hollis back to the *Hunkered Down*. Denny was shown to his room in the same manner. Before Walt could be taken to his room by another armed man, the Spaniard said, "Wait. Señor Ulrich, I would like to have a word with you if you don't mind."

He waited while the crewman exited, closing the door on the way out. When they were alone, The Spaniard sat down in his chair and put his feet up on the table. He lit a Cuban cigar, clasped his hands behind his head and said, "Would you like a cigar?"

"No thanks. I don't smoke," Walt replied cordially.

"You do not have many bad habits, do you?"

"Oh, I have some; I don't always brush my teeth after every meal."

The Spaniard laughed and said, "You are funny. You make a good match for my sister, Walter."

"What are you talking about?' Walt asked in an inno-cent voice.

"Come, come. I am the Captain of this ship. Do you not

think I know where Maria spent last night?"

Walt said in a somber tone, "Then you must also know that Haggarty is not going to let us go. After you're finished with us, we'll all die."

"Tell me you did not hear that from Maria."

"No," said Walt. "She believes big brother will take care of everything."

The Spaniard smiled, but Walt detected a hint of worry in his eyes.

When he spoke, his voice did not seem to have the usual confidence. "You could come along with us. I love having friends along on my little adventures. We will spend the winter in the Caribbean, the summer in the Mediterranean. Who knows where after that?"

"Stealing and pirating as we go?"

"This is not about stealing. We only need enough to maintain our lifestyle."

Walt sighed and said, "I'm sorry, but I can't do that."

"You would make Maria happy."

Walt said, "You and Maria could come with us. Turn Haggerty in. I'm sure none of the others would mind splitting the money with you when they learned the whole story."

The Spaniard frowned. "That is not my style. To me, that sounds boring. Exploring, meeting new friends such as yourself and living life to the utmost is what I have in mind. Sailing the seas, experiencing the finer points of life at the most exclusive seaports in the world ... that is what I see for my future for the next ten, perhaps twenty years." Juan

Chavez drew on his cigar. He exhaled a great cloud of smoke. "The best cigars, the rarest wine from upper echelon wineries, fine food prepared by top flight chefs, this will be my future. And it can also be yours Walter. Adventure by day, exquisite luxury by night." The Spaniard flashed a warm smile. "What do you say?"

"Anyone would be crazy to not want the life you portray. But, that's the easy road, not the best road."

The smile faded from the Spaniard's face.

"If you examine your plan closely, I mean really scrutinize it, you'll see the flaws. You'll be on the run for the rest of your life. Every port you enter could have authorities there waiting for you. When you are out on the town, you'll never know when someone might recognize you."

"I have managed to live fairly worry free for all my adult life," the Spaniard stated.

"But this is different. There are too many lives at stake here. You have a partner that you don't trust. You may have the best intentions, but Haggarty won't let us live. People will come looking. You won't have much peace for the rest of your days."

The Spaniard puffed on his cigar.

After a brief pause, Walt rose from his chair and started for the door. "I should get some sleep." He headed toward the door and added, "Think over what I said Juan. I think you know throwing in with us would be the best thing to do."

"And you give my offer some thought," the Spaniard said in a voice lacking conviction.

"It's a deal," Walt said, trying to stay calm. For the first time in days, he felt a flicker of hope. There was a chance the Spaniard would do what he asked. The life the Spaniard spoke of was a fantasy. With the money derived from this shipwreck, they all could live good lives and not have to worry about looking over their shoulder for the rest of their lives. He needed to talk to Maria. If Walt could influence her, then maybe they could both persuade the Spaniard to do the right thing.

Even though Walt tried to talk the Spaniard out of his plan, he could not help thinking about the life portrayed. Lying in his room aboard *Searcher*, Walt allowed his mind to drift. The life of a jet setter ... what a life it would be. Although he knew it was the wrong decision, it felt good to indulge in a bit of fantasy. Coupled with the idea that he had a chance of talking the Spaniard into coming over to his side, Walt fell off to sleep and slept soundly without waking until dawn.

Chapter Seventeen

The next morning, Walt woke up feeling great. He whistled and sang the Johnny Cash tune 'Ring of Fire' while he prepared for the day. The things that occurred on this vacation previously had him feeling down and not like his usual self. However, he could now see light at the end of the tunnel. Walt figured that he and his friends had a good chance of getting out of this alive, and possibly becoming rich to boot. Besides, as he continued to whistle, Walt thought, if this does not work out I could always become a Johnny Cash impersonator. He smiled and exited the room.

Sometimes, it is a good thing people are unable to see the future. If Walt knew how this day would end up, he may have hummed a tune more fitting for a horror show.

On the way down the aisle, he checked on Brock. His guard waited just outside the door. Brock did not look good. He lay on a bunk with a good portion of his body bandaged, very pale ... sickly ... close to death. His eyes were closed and he appeared to be in a deep sleep. Walt stood over Brock and could not help staring at his friend.

Brock stirred and opened his eyes partially. In a weak voice, he asked, "Are you just going to stand there gawking or are you going to bust me out of here?"

Walt furrowed his brow. Taken back, he was not sure of what to say.

Suddenly, Brock sat up. He appeared as though he was wide-awake. "What's up?" He asked in an urgent whisper.

Walt was taken back again. He said, "You mean you weren't sleeping?"

"Ha! No, I heard someone at the door and thought if I played possum maybe one of the guards would get careless with his weapon. Then I'd jump him and make a jail break."

"You'd jump him?"

"Yea ... but now you're here so what's the plan?"

A wave of astonishment washed over Walt. A few seconds ago, he thought he was losing his old friend. "You mean you're doing OK?"

Brock brushed the question away with a wave of his hand. "I'm in a little pain, but I'm fine. No pain, no gain. The women are going to love my hand-to-hand shark-fighting story; of course, I'll leave your part out. I wouldn't want to embarrass you."

Walt covered his mouth with his hand muffling a good, hearty laugh. He now knew for sure that Brock was recovering fine.

He filled Brock in on his plan to sway Maria and the Spaniard to their side. Of course, Brock wanted to make an immediate escape, but he reluctantly went along with the idea.

Walt left Brock to rest and regain some of his strength.

He met Denny on the deck of the *Hunkered Down.* "I talked to Brock, he's doing better."

"That's good news," Denny answered solemnly.

"Try not to sound so excited."

Denny did not speak. He started to get his gear ready for the dive.

"What's up?" Walt asked.

"What did the Spaniard want to talk about when you were alone with him last night?"

Walt took a quick glance at the Maori who sat on a deck chair fifteen feet away. "Oh, nothing important." Walt stepped close to Denny and whispered, "He may throw in with us. You and I need to talk when we get the chance." He gave Denny a wink and started to get his gear ready.

Lynn came out onto the deck and handed the men bagels.

Walt took a bite from his and said, "Where's Hollis?"

"He's monitoring the radio," said Lynne. "They've disabled our ship to shore radio, but we can still get weather reports on the VHF. There's a tropical storm coming up toward the Bahamas. There's already a small craft warning for Miami and the upper Keys."

Denny asked, "Is it heading for us?"

"They don't know that yet, but it's moving fast. The storm will either turn east and head up the coast or move into the Gulf and straight for us."

Walt asked, "How long if it heads for us?"

"If it heads for us, you can bet things will be pretty

hairy by tomorrow night."

"That's just great!" Denny exclaimed. "A hurricane is all we need."

Lynn said calmly, "Right now it's a tropical storm. It isn't a hurricane yet."

Ensign Walsh stared at the row of monitors and radar screens. He had just finished putting out another alert. Walsh picked up a freshly printed out sheet of paper. The paper contained a report from the National Oceanic and Atmospheric Administration also known as NOAA, based on Blank Key. NOAA was the United States agency responsible for monitoring environmental and climate changes among a vast list of other concerns. After inspecting it for a moment, he walked over and stood beside his commander.

Commander Robbins sat at the radio. From this position in the Coast Guard Station at the old rail yard on Key West, he could keep in contact and direct all water and aircraft under his command.

Robbins was a tall, slender African American. He was in his twenty-second year of service and did not look forward to his pending retirement in a few years. The Coast Guard had been his life. He had served all over the United States and halfway around the world. He now had the dignity and respect of a full commander.

Ensign Walsh waited while Commander Robbins finished his conversation on the radio. Finally, Robbins signed off.

Swiveling in his chair, Robbins looked up at Walsh and said, "What is it?"

"It's official Sir. Wind speed has hit 76 mph. We now have a full-scale hurricane on our hands."

"Does the Spaniard know of the weather situation?" Walt asked.

Lynn stated, "If he does, it didn't come from me or Hollis. We haven't had a chance to talk to him so far today."

"I'm going to talk to him right now." Walt made his way up the gangway to the *Searcher*. As he did, the Maori watched, but offered no resistance. He looked bored. Walt had gotten halfway across the deck when he spotted an aircraft approaching. He stopped and watched as the plane drew closer. The single engine DeHaviland Beaver floatplane banked and came in low for a landing 100 yards off the *Searcher's* port side. The pontoons hit the water and the plane bounced back up. Twice more the plane skimmed off the blue chop of the sea before finally settling down for good. The pilot taxied the floatplane and cut the engine, allowing it to drift close to the much larger sailing vessel.

The Spaniard came on deck followed by Haggarty, and greeted Walt, "Good morning partner."

Haggarty chimed in, "You better get on with the dive, mate." It was more of a threat than a request.

Walt ignored Haggarty and turned to the Spaniard.

"We have bad weather on the way. I was wondering if you were aware of the Tropical Storm that's bearing down on us?"

"Yes, I am aware, and the Tropical Storm has just been upgraded to a Hurricane."

While the men spoke, two crewmen rowed an impeccable black, wooden life boat across to the floatplane.

Haggarty spoke again, "Your job is to dive. We'll take care of the weather."

"You couldn't take care of a stick," Walt spat, noticing his red, swollen nose.

Taking a step toward Walt, Haggarty said, "I can take care of you, mate."

Walt balled his fists.

"Ahoy!" a female voice called. Maria stood in the lifeboat waving. "Ahoy the *Searcher*!" The men watched as Doctor Qeuokas came out of the plane and stepped into the boat. The crewmen rowed Maria and the Doctor to the boarding ladder where they were helped aboard.

"That was exhilarating! The plane handles magnificently," Doctor Qeuokas proclaimed.

"That's right," Walt said. "I remember you talking to Denny about flying at dinner the other night. You're a Doctor and a pilot."

"Yes, I am. I love to fly. I thought I'd fly out here and check on my patient."

"Well you don't have to look very far," came a voice from behind them.

Everyone turned, surprised to see Brock making his way

across the deck on a pair of crutches.

When he reached the others, the Doctor said, "That's an encouraging sign. How do you feel?"

"I'm in a lot of pain Doc."

The Doctor produced two bottles of pills from the pocket of his trousers. "I have brought stronger pain medication and some antibiotics. Have a seat and I'll look at your wounds." He led his patient to a bench where Brock lay down and allowed the Doctor to examine his wounds.

Maria said to The Spaniard, "I came to warn you of the weather. There is a storm coming."

"Yes, I am aware of the storm. We will pull out tonight. You can take some of the silver with you when you leave. We will bring the remainder and meet you at the designated spot." He then turned to the Doctor. "Doctor, how much weight will the plane carry?"

"We should be able to carry fifty bars," the Doctor said, never taking his attention from Brock's foot.

"Good," the Spaniard said. He then turned to Walt and politely said, "We only have one day remaining. May I suggest you get started with the dive?"

When the Saffir-Simpson scale detects wind speed over 74mph, a cyclone is declared a Hurricane. With a full-blown Hurricane approaching, Commander Robbins felt like a dog chasing its tail. It felt like he had 101 things to do. His only consolation was the knowledge that the work he did helped people and saved lives. Already, he had given numerous orders and launched several air and watercraft to ensure the safety of the public.

"Issue a small craft warning," he told Ensign Walsh.

"Right away sir," came Walsh's reply.

"Have all boats and aircraft expand their patrols. I'm worried about refugees making the trip across the straights." This was not Robbins' first hurricane. He knew how these massive storms could turn the ocean into a violent maelstrom. "Any change in direction in the last half an hour?"

"No sir. She's coming up toward the Bahamas and could still go either way."

The fact that the Coast Guard Station on Key West was closer to Havana, Cuba than it was to Miami, Florida made Key West a prime landing spot for refugees.

"With this storm barreling down on us we won't take any chances. A small raft won't stand a chance in a full-blown Hurricane. We're going to need to get everyone off the ocean as soon as possible."

"Aye, Commander. And knowing the situation in Cuba, any persons deciding to come across probably won't even know there's a storm on the way."

"Exactly."

Chapter Eighteen

Walt and Denny had only been down for fifteen minutes when they ran into a problem. They had already found thirty-six cobs when Walt noticed a malfunction. He had no problem inhaling, but he could not expel the spent air. His mouthpiece was not functioning properly. Quickly, he tapped Denny on the shoulder, pointed up and started kicking for the surface dropping the mesh bag that held the gold cobs. His lungs burned and muscles screamed when, at last, he broke the surface with a gasp. Spitting the mouthpiece out, he took great breaths of air.

Denny followed close behind. "What is it," he asked.

"Mouthpiece ... broke ... I couldn't breathe," Walt said between breaths.

"Are you alright?"

Walt nodded. "I will be. Let's get back aboard the boat."

Walt and Denny climbed aboard the *Hunkered Down* where the Maori waited to meet them. "What's going on? Why are you back so soon?"

Walt explained what had happened with the mouthpiece. The Maori pointed at Walt and ordered, "You, re-place your gear." He pointed to Denny next. "You, go back down."

Walt and Denny exchanged disgusted glances. Walt said, "I'll be right behind you."

Denny went over the side for another dive. Walt had barely begun replacing his gear when Maria shouted from the deck of the sailing ship above, "Walt, would you please come up here for a moment?"

Walt took his swim fins off so that he could walk on the deck. Winking at the Maori, he headed up the gangway still wearing his wetsuit. He found the Spaniard, Bonita and Haggarty along the port rail talking to the Doctor, who already sat in the lifeboat. Brock still lay on the bench. Maria stood in the center of the deck with a warm smile. Walt walked to her.

"I am leaving now Walt, probably for good," Maria said. She hesitated before pleading, "Come with us."

"First you steal my innocence. Then you steal my money. And now you want me to come along with you?"

Maria laughed. "You were as innocent as a boy caught with his hand in a cookie jar."

Walt shook his head. "I can't come along," he said in a sober tone.

Maria hesitated. Then she reached up, wrapped her arms around Walt, and gave him a full kiss. When they parted, she looked serious, but only for a second. The smile returned to her face and she regained her jauntiness. Without another word, she turned and walked away.

"Adios brother. See you soon," she called to the Spaniard as she climbed into the waiting lifeboat along with Doctor Qeuokas and Bonita.

A crewman rowed the boat across the short expanse of ocean to the floatplane. Walt watched as Maria, Bonita and the Doctor boarded the plane. A few seconds later, the engine coughed twice and roared to life. The Doctor turned the craft into the wind. As the plane picked up speed, bouncing on the growing swells, Walt saw Maria through the open side window. Her long, black hair blew in the wind. She was waving and shouting, "Woo-hoo! Good bye Walt!" As the plane picked up speed Maria's voice was lost, carried away on the rising wind.

The plane lifted off and began to climb. Over the fading noise of the engine, Walt heard Brock's voice, "Boy, you really broke her heart."

Walt turned and found Brock leaning on his crutches.

With a sly grin, Brock said, "You know ... you really should learn how to let a woman down easy."

Walt said, "Yea, and I should've let the sharks have you." However, he could not stop a smile from creeping in.

The Spaniard and Haggarty started walking across the deck toward the doorway that led to the ship's interior when the Spaniard stopped and said, "Give me one minute. I'll be right with you."

Haggarty continued. The Spaniard walked over to Walt and Brock. He glanced around nervously and in a low voice said, "I have thought it over and decided that you are right."

Walt was surprised. He glanced at Brock who looked confused.

The Spaniard continued, "I have not had a chance to talk to Maria, but what I want to do, she will also do. I want to do what you said, turn Haggarty in ... if I am not persecuted."

"That's terrific," Walt said. "After all, from what Maria has told me, you were coerced by Haggarty."

"I have your word. I will not be persecuted?"

"Absolutely," Walt said in earnest.

The Spaniard asked, "What about the others? Will they go along with it?"

Walt looked at his friend and asked, "Brock?"

Brock shrugged his shoulders and said, "Yea, sure."

"OK. Then just as you speak for Maria, I can speak for Denny, Hollis, and Captain Meyers."

"I have your word?" the Spaniard asked.

"You have my word."

"It's a deal." The Spaniard looked around. "We cannot act now. Make another dive Walt. When you come up for lunch, I will have my crew ready. We will overpower Haggarty and his mate and end this situation. I should go now. Be ready when you surface again"

Walt kicked straight for the bottom and headed for Denny. Adrenaline pumped through his veins and he had struggled to keep his excitement from the Maori while he prepared for the dive. Now that Walt was under water, he could hardly wait to fill Denny in on what was going on.

He found Denny digging into the ocean floor with a trowel. Denny had not noticed Walt's approach and when Walt tapped him on the shoulder, he swung around with the trowel pointed at his chest. Walt backed off and raised his hands trying to calm his friend. When Denny realized that it was Walt, he relaxed. He lowered the trowel and stared with a scowl.

Walt still felt jubilant. He urgently motioned for Denny to follow. Walt led Denny to a level stretch of seabed that was undisturbed by their excavation. Using his finger, Walt began to print in the gravel. **The Spaniard is with us.** Walt gave Denny time to read what he printed before printing again. **Hag is finished be ready when we go up.** Walt waited for Denny to read what he had printed. When he did, Denny looked at Walt and nodded. Walt returned the nod.

Walt swept his hands over the bottom and brushed away the message. He pointed to the site where they were digging for and finding the gold cobs. Both divers swam slowly, silently back to that spot and went back to work.

Walt and Denny worked until their air was almost gone. They added fifty-eight gold coins to the mesh bag, bringing the total to ninety-four. On purpose, they surfaced fifty yards away from the two boats.

The men trod water as they removed their regulators. In a barely audible voice, Walt said, "The Spaniard and his crew are going to jump Haggarty and the Maori. Be careful, stay out of the line of fire."

Denny began to swim for the boat. "Understood. Don't worry; I'll be hiding in a corner."

As they drew near the boats, Walt could see people moving about on the black sailing vessel. Because he was in the water, looking up and across the deck of the *Hunkered Down*, he could only see the people from the chest up. Walt could make out the crewmember with the thin mustache, Haggarty, and the Maori. He could not hear their voices, but it seemed they were involved in an intense argument.

Walt reached the ladder and began to climb. "Here we go again, partner."

When the men reached the deck, they found the *Hunkered Down* abandoned. Hurriedly, they removed their air tanks and fins and climbed the gangway to the *Searcher*.

As soon as they reached the deck, the divers froze in their tracks. Walt looked at Denny, who stood as still as a stone with his mouth agape. Walt turned his attention back to the unbelievable scene before him.

Haggarty stood before the men. He swung his pistol toward Walt and Denny when they came on deck. He held it level on them now. Lynne and Hollis sat on the bench, their hands and feet tied, their eyes filled with horror. The Maori pointed a shotgun at the lone crewman on deck. In the center of the wooden deck, the Spaniard lay in a pool of blood. He had a bullet hole in his chest and one in the center of his forehead.

Walt stared in shock. An overwhelming sense of dread spread over him. As he stared, he knew for certain, without a doubt, the Spaniard was dead. Without the Spaniard to control Haggerty and the Maori, he knew that he and his friends would be too.

Soon...very soon.

———

No one at the diner had seen Hollis for a few days. Likewise, when he asked the neighbors. As Art stood in front of Hollis's home, he thought over the events that led to this dead end. First, he got a call from Hollis James. Hollis says his friend Walter Ulrich needs him to come right away. He knows Walt would not ask for Art unless there was something wrong. Walter and his friends are diving out on the open ocean, a million and one things could go wrong.

Next, Hollis is supposed to meet Art at the Airport. He does not show up. Calls to his phone go right to voicemail, something Hollis James's phone never does. No one has seen him for a few days and he does not appear to be home. There is no sign of his truck. Either something has happened to Hollis, Art determines, or he is out there with Walter and the others.

He must do something.

"Why don't you stay here for a second, I want to check out the house," Art said to Barb.

"Are you sure you don't want to call the police first?"

Art shook his head. "I want to try this first. Let's see if we can figure out what's going on."

Barb said, "OK, but be careful."

Art flashed that infectious smile. "Besides, you know

how the saying goes. You had better do something when you're young. If you don't, you'll have to lie when you're old."

The space under the stairs did not relinquish the house key that Art searched for. Next, he tried under a dilapidated flowerpot and got the same results. Art ran his hand along the sill over the front door, finding only dust. Without much conviction, he lifted the rubber floor mat in front of the door. To his surprise, he found the key. Art wondered who but Hollis would hide a key in such an obvious place?

Art opened the door and went inside, hoping not to find a grotesque murder scene. He did not. Nothing looked out of place. Art thought about wearing gloves so his fingerprints would not interfere with an investigation. However, he never really believed that Hollis was here. He was out on the ocean with Walt.

Striding over to a cluttered desk, Art searched for any link to the whereabouts of his friends. He did not have long to wait. On the desktop sat an Apple lap top computer, a fax machine, a copy machine and a telephone with a landline. Next to the phone lay an open leather binder. The heading at the top of the page read *Walter Ulrich Expedition.*

When Art scrolled down the page until he came upon coordinates. He hurried to the doorway and called for Barb to come in. Side by side, they studied the page. Art tore a piece of paper from a notebook and copied the coordinates. He did not find anything else of assistance.

"There's not a hell of a lot here. No name of the boat they're using ... nothing," Art said.

Barb said, "No, it looks as though he hurriedly scribbled down the coordinates and that's it. More than likely, he keeps full records on his computer."

"Can you get into it?"

"No," Barb said. "You'd need the password. A tech guy could do it."

"We don't have time for that," Art said, leading his wife out to the front porch. "I'm going to find a boat and go look for them."

"What about the storm?"

Art glanced at the sky. "I'll have plenty of time to get out to their position and back.'

"The police can crack his laptop for sure."

"Yes, but again, I don't think we have the time. Look," Art said in a patient tone, "until we know more about what's going on and where they are, I don't think we'll get a whole lot of help. With the storm heading this way, the authorities have their hands full."

"I want to come along."

"I understand, but we'll be better served if you stay here. While I'm heading out, you can contact the authorities and fill them in on everything we talked about."

Barb took a deep breath. A look of worry appeared in her eyes. In a concerned voice, she pleaded, "Be careful Art."

"My friends could be in trouble. I have to go." With a reassuring smile, he added, "Don't worry Babe. At least I won't lack for exciting stories to tell when I grow old."

Barb drove the rental vehicle to the police station. Art walked the short distance to the marina. Although the attendant behind the counter insisted he had mental health issues, Art used his personal credit card to rent a boat for the day. The two one-hundred dollar bills Art slid into his hand helped convince the attendant that the storm was not that bad, and would not arrive anytime soon.

The twenty-foot Boston Whaler was equipped for a day of pleasure boating and not much else. Art did not mind. Despite what he told the attendant, he felt time was growing short. Within half an hour of separating from Barb at Hollis's house, he was piloting the boat out of the marina. Ignoring the strange looks from those coming into harbor from the storm, he jammed the throttle to its stops as soon as he cleared the no-wake zone. Mounting swells and a darkening sky to the east gave the open ocean an ominous look.

Chapter Nineteen

Haggarty cracked a malevolent smile at Walt and said, "Now that the Spaniard's out of the way, things will go a might smoother." Motioning toward the crewman with the thin mustache, he said, "Take that one below and lock him up with the rest of the crew." Almost as an afterthought, he added, "And bring that piece of shark bait up on deck. I'll get rid of that loudmouth while I'm at it."

Walt did not speak. He was dumbfounded.

The Maori led the crewman below deck.

Haggarty laughed and said, "What's the matter boys, cat got your tongue?"

Walt still could not believe what he saw. "What happend here?"

"I made a business decision. I just increased my share to 100%. Who needs that two-bit, wannabe pirate?" Haggarty said coldly. "I'm sorry you missed it. I would have loved for you to watch the Spaniard die. No worries, you can watch while I put the cripple's lights out."

As if on cue, Brock was forced out onto the deck at gunpoint. The Maori led him to the spot where the Spaniard lay. Haggarty stood behind him and began to raise his pistol. He wore a smile. Brock showed no emotion, as if he had accepted his fate.

Walt snapped out of his stupor. He still carried the mesh bag. Opening the drawstrings, Walt took out one of the gold coins. "You might want to look at this," Walt said, flipping the coin to Haggarty.

Haggarty palmed the coin, rubbing his fingers over the surface. There is something witchy about holding gold in your hand. Haggarty's eyes took on a faraway look.

When Walt spoke, his tone sounded enticing, "Gold cobs. There are a hundred more in this bag." He took a quick, sudden step and with every ounce of strength, slung the bag as far as he could out over the ocean. A handful of coins spilled out of the open bag and splashed as they landed along the waves. When the mesh bag hit the water, it sank immediately.

"What are you doing?" Haggarty screamed.

Walt stood his ground, not answering.

Brock said, "If you're going to shoot me, then do it. Stop jerking me around."

Haggarty turned toward Brock and said, "Oh, I am going to shoot you."

"Walt stated, "You do that and you can kiss that gold good-bye." He had Haggarty's full attention so he continued, "Here's the deal. I'll dive again for the gold, but you must let them go. I'm not bringing up another ounce if you're going to kill us anyway."

Haggarty thought about this proposition for a moment. "They go, you stay."

"That's right."

Brock swiveled on his crutches and said, "No way. I'm staying ... "

"Knock it off, Brock," Walt said. To Haggarty he said, "Put them on the *Hunkered Down* and anchor a mile away. When I finish diving, you leave and they can come and get me." Haggarty made no reply. Walt continued, "Listen, I'm tired and I've had enough of this. Truthfully, I don't care if you shoot me right now. This is my only offer, take it or leave it."

After she talked to the police, Barb headed straight for the Coast Guard Station at the old rail yard. Not that she did not trust the police, but Barb did not hold high expectations for them to provide any useful assistance ... at least not in the immediate future. She hoped the Coast Guard would produce different results.

After she explained who she was and she might know of a situation involving missing persons, and boats out on the ocean, a seaman escorted her to a waiting room. The dimensions of the room matched those of a small cubicle. Barb took a seat on the lone metal chair in the room.

She did not wait long.

In less than five minutes, a tall man entered the room and introduced himself, "Hello Mam, I'm Commander Robbins."

Barb stood and introduced herself.

Commander Robbins waited patiently while she explained the situation. In a compassionate, but firm voice, he said, "I understand your concern Mrs. Kendall. Believe me; we will do whatever we can to locate your husband and missing friend, but ... "

Barb raised an eyebrow, "But?" she interrupted.

Robbins sighed. "Search and rescue is what we do here. But," he continued, "we have a huge area to cover."

"So, my husband isn't a priority."

"Never said that."

"Are you going to help me?"

"Of course," Robbins said. "I simply cannot deploy a great deal of resources for this situation. There is a Cutter making ready to depart as we speak. I'll send it to the coordinates you've provided."

Barb felt a measure of relief. "Thank you, Commander."

Robbins turned to leave. "You welcome Ma'am. As I said, this is what we do."

As the Commander reached for the door, Barb added, "There's one more thing."

"Yes?"

"I'm going along."

Commander Robbins stopped and stared at Barb with a frown. When he saw the look of determination in her eyes, he knew she would not be put off.

Walt retrieved the mesh bag full of gold coins first. He swam the bag to the dig site and dropped it beside the area where he and Denny had been working. He picked up a trowel and began to dig. Once he used up most of his air, Walt had found an additional 60 gold cobs. He placed these in a second bag. The weight of the bags made it too heavy for Walt to carry them to the surface. He attached a rope to each bag. As he slowly rose to the surface, he played out slack from the coils of rope in his hands.

Brock, Denny, Lynn, and Hollis had been placed aboard the *Hunkered Down*. She lay at anchor about a mile off the other boat's starboard bow. The minute he broke the surface, Walt pulled his facemask off. He felt relieved to find the *Hunkered Down* anchored in her same position.

Haggarty stood at the controls of his yacht. When Walt waved, he brought the boat up alongside. Walt held the ends of the ropes up above the rising swells for Haggarty to see and called, "There are 2 bags of gold on the other end of these ropes." He threw the ends over the side of Haggarty's boat. "Pull them up and they're yours."

"Come aboard Walter."

Walt glanced at the *Hunkered Down* a mile away, and then at *Searcher* which rode the swells only about fifty yards away. He did not have a choice.

"All right, but when my friends see me climb aboard, and I'm sure they're watching, they'll go for help. You won't catch them."

Haggarty placed his hand on top of the pistol tucked into the waistband of his trousers. "Just come aboard, mate."

Walt climbed the ladder to the yacht's main deck where he found Haggarty pointing the pistol in his direction. In his free hand, Haggarty held the radio mike. While Walt removed his air tanks, Haggarty keyed the mike and spoke, "All right Jonna, Bring them back."

Walt watched in amazement as the *Hunkered Down* started to move in their direction. He felt ridiculous. He couldn't believe he'd been deceived. The Maori must have gotten aboard without his noticing.

The yacht passed alongside the *Hunkered Down.* Walt saw Jonna the Maori at the helm. Haggarty and the Maori exchanged nods as they passed. The *Hunkered Down* continued until it came up alongside Haggarty's yacht.

Haggarty ordered Walt to place his hands behind his back. Walt vowed silently not to go down without a fight. When Haggarty attempted to fasten a heavy-duty plastic wire tie around his wrists, Walt began to spin around to face him. However, years in intelligence and espionage paid off for Haggarty. He was ready and before Walt could completely turn around, he landed a blow with the butt of the pistol to the top of Walt's head.

Walt saw stars. The last thing he noticed was the floorboards rising to hit him in the face before he blacked out.

Art Kendall eased back on the throttle slowing the boat to 10 mph. This was the spot Hollis had marked, but all he saw a mile and a half in the distance was the sleek, black, sailing ship and a smaller pleasure yacht. He searched the horizon with a pair of binoculars and saw not another single boat. What a beautiful work of craftsmanship he thought, returning his gaze to the sailing vessel.

The smaller watercraft was coming up alongside the black ship on the far side and out of Art's sight. He searched the increasing blue swells again and again saw no other boats. He swung the binoculars back just as his boat drifted back, bobbing past the black boat's stern. This angle allowed Art to see both sides of the black sailing ship. The stern of the yacht came into view again. Brazen gold letters painted across the stern pronounced the name of the yacht. *LEXICON*, Art read the name aloud. As he drifted, the *Hunkered Down* came into better view. Even at this distance, Art saw that she was an old fishing boat refitted for work, most likely diving. Lines moored her, along with a second boat, to the Black ship.

Art trained the binoculars on a gangway which led from the sailing ship to the second boat. He could not make out the faces but he was sure he saw people being led across the gangway from the smaller boat to the much larger vessel. Art flexed his knees to remain steady on the pitching boat. As he stared through the binoculars, the activity on the gangway became clear. He saw a dark man with a gun herding several persons with their hands tied across the gangway.

Art had seen enough. This had to be Hollis, Walt, and the others. He thought about calling the Coast Guard on the radio, but the call would be heard over the open airwaves. He guessed that someone from the mysterious black vessel might be listening. Art did not like cellular phones. With the smart phone design, he felt people were slaves to high tech. Many people he knew could not stand to be more than a few feet or seconds from their phones night and day. Art preferred to use a satellite phone. He did not need all the bells and whistles, but he could make or take a call from just about anywhere in the world.

He picked up his Global Star Satellite phone and called Barb.

Commander Robbins had walked Barb to the dock where the crew almost had the Coast Guard Cutter ready to go out to sea. "Are you sure you want to do this? It could get rough out there."

"My husband's out there," Barb said. With that, her phone rang. She looked at it and said, "That's him now." Barb put the phone to her ear. "Art, are you all right?"

"I'm fine," he assured her. He got right to the point. "I'm at the coordinates that Hollis had written down. Where are you?"

"I'm at the Coast Guard Station."

"Good. Walt, Hollis and the rest are in trouble. Get the Coast Guard out here as soon as possible. I'm ditching the boat I rented so if the Coast Guard spots it, tell them not to worry; I'll be on Walt's boat."

"How will you get to Walt's boat?" Barb asked.

"I'm going to swim."

"Swim," she repeated.

"Yes. Look, I'm not exactly sure what's going on here, but I can tell there's not much time."

"OK Art, I'll get the Coast Guard there right away. Be careful."

"Outstanding as always dear. And, I will be careful, try not to worry."

That was like telling her to try not to breathe.

Barb relayed the information to Commander Robbins. She started for the Cutter and said, "I'll talk to you when I get back."

"No, you won't," Robbins said, "because I'm coming along."

Chapter Twenty

Art made a quick decision. He removed his sneakers and peeled off his T-shirt. He emptied his pockets ... car keys, change, and wallet. He laid the contents on the table. Art noticed a pair of swim fins along with some wetsuits and various other scuba gear in the corner. Picking up the fins, he made his way along the starboard side of the boat. Behind the cabin and away from prying eyes, wearing only a pair of shorts, Art adjusted the fins to fit his feet, and put them on. Without a second thought, he took several deep breaths and slipped over the side.

The boat continued drifting on the current at a slow pace, leaving Art alone in the ocean water. He had not thought about current until he began to swim. A slight current ran from Art's left to right. Wearing the fins, Art knew he could swim the mile and a half. The swells were now up to over three feet. Although this made for a more difficult swim, he believed the swells would help to conceal his approach. He set out swimming the American crawl at a steady pace, breathing every three strokes. Art compensated for the current by angling twenty degrees to the black ship's port side.

Art swam steadily until he was within a half mile of the black ship. He stopped swimming and trod water while he gathered his bearings. The current had been pushing him to his right. On this course, he would miss the boats entirely. Art did not want to think about the consequences he would face if the current pushed him past the boats. He started swimming again, this time at a harder angle. Art swam hard now, using powerful kicks and strong strokes. Due to the strong current and some fatigue, it took longer for him to cover the last half mile than it did the first full mile.

Finally, twenty yards from the looming black hull Art halted his strokes. He found himself only slightly to the vessel's port side. Art used an easy breaststroke to close the remaining gap. Swimming around to the starboard side, he slipped past the yacht and up to the next boat. While he clung to the dive platform and caught his breath, Art read the name painted across the stern. *Hunkered Down.* He saw dive equipment strewn around on the deck. Underwater metal detectors stood propped up in one corner. Art knew he had made the right decision. This had to be the dive boat Walt and others were using.

Art did not see anyone on either of the smaller boats, nor could he see anyone aboard the much larger sailing vessel. Although, from his position at sea level, he found it impossible to completely see the sailing vessel's deck. Climbing aboard the *Hunkered Down,* he pulled his fins off and set out to make a quick search of the vessel. The lengthy swim made Art's legs feel like jelly. It took a moment for him to adjust, but he soon grew accustomed to being out of the water. Suddenly, he heard two loud bangs, then two more. The shots came from inside the hull of the black sailing ship. They sounded like gunshots. 'Oh no,' he thought. 'I hope I'm not too late.'

Not finding anyone aboard the dive boat, he hurried up the gangway to the deck of the *Searcher*. Art stepped through the open doorway to the bridge and found the area unoccupied. A bump came from the deck outside. He eased his head around the door. He saw a large man on the rear deck. The man sported orange hair and an orange mustache.

Ernst Haggarty was busy rigging a block and tackle to the sway arm. Heavy ropes led from the block and tackle to a cargo net. When Haggarty pulled the ropes, the net would draw closed and hoist the cargo. Bars of silver made up the cargo. The man, Art reasoned, was preparing to transfer the cargo from the dive boat to the yacht. Art pulled his head back inside the bridge. He noticed a stairway leading down. Quickly he descended the stairs, taking two at a time.

The Maori admired his work. The four shots from the twelve-gauge shotgun had made a nice hole in the hull. Seawater rushed in through a hole one-foot in diameter.

The damage would sink the boat, but should give them enough time to remove the treasure ... if they hurried. He exited the compartment leaving the door open. Climbing the stairs to the cabin deck, he reached the top and broke into a trot. He went through the hallway and into the salon, covering the distance in only seconds. He continued trotting until he ran smack into a hard object at the base of the stairs. The powerful collision jarred the shotgun from his hands. The gun slid under a sofa and ended up along the far wall.

The Maori stumbled back a few steps. He stared at the solidly built man before him. The man looked dangerous. Cocking his head, he wondered who this wet man wearing only a pair of shorts was.

The collision knocked Art down and back into the stairway. He shook his head to clear the cobwebs and focused on the dark man who stood before him. As he sprang to his feet, Art demanded, "Where's Hollis? Where is Walt Ulrich?"

"They are dead and so are you," the Maori replied, dropping into a fighting crouch.

Art did not think about the answer. If they were dead, there was nothing he could do. If they were alive, he would have to get past this man before he could help them. Art put his fists up and the two men began to circle. The Maori's curly black hair and tattooed face made for a menacing sight. Looking into the eyes of his opponent, Art could see he was a deadly man. Art knew ... he just knew, this would be a fight to the death.

The Maori made the first move. Feinting a right cross, he lashed out with a kick aimed at Art's knee. Art moved quickly however, and he took a step back. Instead of connecting with Art's kneecap, the kick landed on his calf. Art felt sharp pain shooting through his calf, but he knew that no major damage had been done. The Maori had made a quick, difficult move. If his foot would have connected with Art's kneecap it probably would have shattered. That would have been an early end to the fight and to his life, Art realized as they began to circle again.

Art moved first this time taking two straight jabs at his opponent's nose. The Maori moved away with ease. The jabs never came close. 'Not only does this guy look tough,' Art thought, 'the son of a bitch has skill.'

The Maori came at Art with a series of kicks and punches. Art also fended them off easily, too easily, he thought. His opponent was either testing him or setting him up. His instinct proved right. The Maori attacked once more, this time for real. Art blocked the first two kicks but did not see the straight right hand until it was almost too late. He moved his head to the side, but the Maori's knuckles grazed the side of his head opening a shallow cut from the corner of his right eye all the way to his ear. Art struck back with a short, left hook to the ribs. The blow did not have enough energy to do much harm, it did however, cause the Maori to miss his next punch, a left hand that sailed wide. Art brought his foot up and gave a short, quick kick to the man's midsection. The move was more of a shove than a kick and it put some distance between them.

The men circled.

The dark man shook his head to clear the long, black, curly hair from in front of his eyes. A thin smile formed on his lips.

Art Kendall felt blood from the cut on his face dripping onto his bare chest. He limped slightly as he circled. As he kept his blue eyes locked on the other man, he saw the smile. He knew the man felt confident, and rightly so. Art had landed a few blows but they were ineffectual. Meanwhile, he was taking a beating. At this rate, he would not last long.

The Maori closed the gap between them in a flash. A flurry drove Art back, but he blocked every kick and punch. This time, they did not separate. Art lowered his head and rushed the other man tackling him. The men hit the floor with Art on top. However, the Maori was extremely agile and escaped Art's grasp. He began to stand up when Art landed a haymaker of a left hook. The force of the blow spun the Maori around. He hit the floor, rolled, and sprang right back to his feet.

Art went right at him. First throwing a right cross as a decoy, and then a straight left jab. The jab connected with the Maori's nose with a crack, snapping his head back. Art threw another jab and then a right cross while his opponent lashed out with a kick aimed at Art's groin. The blows from both men landed simultaneously but both missed their intended mark.

Art's right was intended to break the man's jaw, but it fell a hair short. Pieces of teeth flew across the room as his fist drove the man's head sideways. At the same instant, the Maori's kick landed with tremendous force. The kick missed Art's groin, but landed high on his right thigh, buckling his leg. Art staggered backwards a few steps. The searing pain in his leg felt almost unbearable. He felt nauseated and thought he might pass out. Had this been a boyhood fight in a schoolyard, Art would have gladly thrown in the towel at this point. However, this was more than a testosterone-fueled battle of egos. Art knew there was no stopping. He would have to win or he would surely die.

The Maori stood bent over with his hands on his knees. His eye was starting to swell and blood poured from his nose. He spat blood and pieces of teeth onto the floor. Art's head cleared at last. He saw an opportunity to put an end to the fight. He attempted to take a step, but his leg gave out. Something was seriously wrong. He did not merely have a bruise or a strained muscle. As Art hobbled along unable to put any weight on his leg, he knew the kick must have fractured bone.

The Maori straightened up and smiled through his smashed mouth. Art knew he was in a bad situation. The fight had been even, but with Art's immobility, he was at a huge disadvantage.

The Maori attacked with a series of punches and kicks. One by one, Art blocked them until a powerful and well-placed kick landed on his right thigh. The kick landed in the same spot as the previous one. This time, Art heard as well as felt the bone break. He went down like a house of cards. As he lay on the wood floor, his heart sank. He was beaten. Art was not afraid to die. His entire life he had met every adverse situation head on, but this time he felt as though he had let himself down. More importantly, he felt as though he had let Barb down. Would she ever know what had become of him? What would become of her? As Art watched the Maori move in for the kill, he wished he could see his wife one more time.

The Maori stalked in slowly. His face showed no emotion as he raised his leg to deliver one final, decisive blow to Art's throat. Suddenly, the boat lurched. While the fight took place, seawater had been rushing into the engine room. Three feet of water now flooded the engine room and water flowed into the companionway and into the other compartments on the lower deck. The weight of the water caused the boat to shift and list to its starboard side. The movement of the boat caught the Maori off guard. The deck went out from under him and he fell, landing flat on his back. His head hit the teak deck with a crack.

From where he lay on his back, Art did not know what made the man fall and he was not going to wait around to find out. Before the Maori had a chance to get up, Art was on him, clamping his arm around the man's throat. Art tightened his grip, locking the Maori in a chokehold. He maintained his vice-like grip as the man thrashed about. The Maori gave it everything he had, but it was no use. Art held on. He held on and he held on squeezing the life from his opponent. For several long minutes after the Maori stopped breathing, Art continued to hold tight. Finally, he eased up and released his grip, pushing the lifeless body away.

The boat listed harder to starboard now. Art took a few seconds to regain his composure and then began to rise on his good leg. He never felt the bullet enter through his right shoulder blade. He did however, feel the bullet exit through his chest. He also felt the tremendous impact, knocking him from his feet.

Art lay on the deck in shock. He knew he had been shot. He saw a man standing at the bottom of the stairway. He was the same man Art had seen earlier on deck. The big man with the orange hair and thick mustache had a wild look in his eyes. "You killed Jonna!" he screamed raising his gun and pulling the trigger.

Art heard the bullet sing past, inches from his head. Turning his head away instinctively, he noticed an object under the couch. Art reach under the couch and grabbed the object with his right hand. At the same time, a slug tore through his left forearm.

Haggarty was firing wildly. Art brought the shotgun out from underneath the couch. Another bullet whizzed past, and then one hit art high in his left shoulder. In a move of desperation, Art raised the shotgun, pointed, and pulled the trigger all in one motion. The kick of the 12-gauge distorted his vision for an instant. When his vision cleared, he saw the big orange haired man lying in the stairway. Art's shot had been on target. Several pellets had hit Haggarty in the head, neck and chest. Blood spilled onto the stairs and floor. Haggarty's eyes remained wide open. He was stone dead.

Art slumped on the floor with his back propped up against the couch. The boat lurched again and listed harder. Art knew he should search for his friends, but he did not have the energy. Instead, Art Kendall closed his eyes and saw images of his wife.

Chapter Twenty-One

Walter Ulrich blinked his eyes open. All he saw was white. His ears rang and his head thumped. Gradually, his vision returned and he found himself lying on his back facing a bright blue sky. He looked at his hands and saw that a plastic wire tie bound them together.

Walt had no idea of where he was. Trying to stand, he found everything moving. His vision swam. He lay down once more. In a moment, the dizziness passed, but the movement did not let up. Walt glanced around and found himself on a boat. The boat bobbed on the waves. That is where the movement came from. He wore a wet suit, his hands were tied, but he had no recollection of how he came to find himself in this situation.

He attempted to stand again. This time he successfully struggled to his feet. When Walt saw the black hull of the *Searcher*, his memory began to come back. He was on board Haggarty's yacht. The facts were fuzzy, but Walt knew his friends were aboard the ominous black pirate ship and they were in trouble. *Searcher* did not appear the way Walt remembered. Her hull showed a definite cant to the starboard side. Gray-black smoke rose from her decks.

Walt found a knife and cut his hands free. He peeled off his wetsuit and, wearing only shorts, climbed the rope ladder to the Blank. He had the presence of mind to take the knife along, knowing he might need to use it. Slowly, while he stood on the deck of the luxurious yacht, Walt's memory returned. He remembered the double cross by Haggarty and the Maori. His head still ached, but the ringing in his ears stopped. Walt remembered the Spaniard, the treasure ... everything. He did not remember smoke pouring from below deck. Walt could not have known about Haggarty firing wildly and one of the errant bullets from his gun traveling through the salon wall. One of the bullets that was meant for Art. The lead slug penetrated the wall and ruptured a propane line. Fire had already spread through two decks.

Walt found no one above deck. He searched the bridge and found that it too was empty. Taking the stairway leading below deck, he came upon a grizzly scene. Haggarty lay on his back at the bottom of the stairs. His lifeless eyes stared at the ceiling. His orange hair was his only recognizable feature. From his nose to his mid-section, he looked as though he had been through a meat grinder. Walt bent down and picked up Haggarty's pistol. He stuck the gun into the waistband of his shorts.

Next, he stepped over the body and into the salon. Blood splatters and pools covered most of the salon floor. The Maori lay dead on the deck, his skin already beginning to turn blue. Then, he saw him. Sitting on the floor slumped against the couch was his friend Art Kendall.

Walt was amazed to see his friend and at the same time, he felt saddened to see him in this condition. Cuts and bruises adorned Art's face. Blood seeped from at least three bullet wounds.

When Walt knelt beside him, Art opened his eyes and croaked, "Walt, you're alive."

"Yea, I'm alive. Where are the others?"

"Haven't seen them," Art said in a weak voice. "Go. There isn't much time. Find them."

Walt knew his friend was in bad shape and he felt a terrible guilt. He took some cloth from behind the bar and bandaged Art's wounds the best he could. "Hang on Art. I'll have you out of here in no time." He did not want to leave his friend, but he had to search for the others. 'I won't let him die,' he vowed, 'I won't let any of them die.'

Walt started checking the cabins. The first two were empty. He found the third cabin door locked. Walt used the knife to pry the door open. He found Brock, Denny, Lynne, and Hollis inside and alive. Not wasting any time, Walt used the knife to cut the wire ties that bound their wrists and ankles.

"Boy, are we glad to see you," Brock said.

"What's going on?" Denny asked.

Walt shook his head and said, "There's no time. This boat is on fire and I think she's sinking. Art's in the salon, we need to help him to the *Hunkered Down*."

When Walt freed everyone and they each went on his or

her way to the salon, he went down the companionway in the opposite direction. Smoke poured into the companion-way. The vessel would not stay afloat for long. Walt found all the remaining cabins empty until he came to the last one. Prying open the locked door, Walt stepped inside and found *Searcher's* entire 12-man crew. Each crewmember had his or her hands and feet bound.

Walt freed the man with the thin mustache first. Hand-ing him the knife, Walt said, "This boat is going down. Get everyone out and aboard Haggarty's yacht."

"Haggarty's the man responsible for tying us up. Where is he?" The man asked.

"He's dead." Walt replied, taking the pistol from his waistband. "And anyone who causes any trouble will also die. Do you understand?"

"I understand señor," the man said in a somber tone. "You will have no more trouble with us."

Walt rose and exited the cabin. His head had not totally cleared from the blow he had taken earlier. As he hurried down the companionway, he thought, 'You know, I never did get that guy's name.'

When Walt reached the salon, he found Denny and Hol-lis carrying Art. They had already dragged Haggarty's body away from the stairwell and were just beginning to take Art up the stairs. Brock was already above deck. Lynn stood in the center of the salon. Blood and death surround-ed the Captain as she imagined what terrible things went on here. She turned to Walt with tears welling up in her eyes. Lynn's bottom lip quivered and she said in a cracked voice, "He came."

The enormity of what Art had done started to sink in. Walt nodded, "The pact."

"But look what happened to him," Lynn said breathlessly. The tears flowed down her face. "What kind of a man would do that?"

Walt simply said, "A hero. My friend."

———————

The crew made it aboard the yacht. Walt knew they were not going anywhere, because he had taken the keys. The rest had gotten aboard the dive boat. They were not going anywhere either because the Maori had her keys in his pants pocket. The best any of them could do was to cut the lines and allow the boats to drift free.

Within minutes of the survivors abandoning *Searcher*, they saw flames rising through the deck. Ten minutes later, the hull broke in half and the pirate ship went to the bottom.

For a second, Hollis feared the suction created by the sinking ship would pull them under, but that did not happen. Haggarty's yacht and their bulky dive boat were too large to be pulled under.

———————

From her position in the Rigid Inflatable Boat or R.I.B., Barb noticed that the smoke had stopped rising. She knew whatever had been burning had probably sank.

As the high-speed vessel bounced over the waves, Commander Robbins yelled above the roar of the Honda twin 225 horsepower engines, "Don't worry Mrs. Kendall, we'll be there in no time."

Despite the commander's reassurance, Barb felt very worried. She had a bad feeling. She felt as though she knew something was wrong.

Ten minutes later, the R.I.B. slowed and stopped between the yacht and the *Hunkered Down*. The two boats had drifted sixty yards apart. Hollis called, "Over here. We need a doctor." As the R.I.B. pulled alongside, Hollis recognized Barb. His jaw dropped and he stammered, "B ... Barb, what are you doing here?" Tears began to run down the wrinkles in his face.

The look on his face told Barb her fears were well founded. "Where is he, Hollis?" she asked in a calm voice.

"In the cabin."

Barb said to Robbins, "I'm going over." Without waiting for a reply, she leapt from the Coast Guard inflatable boat to the deck of the *Hunkered Down*.

As she started to make her way to the cabin, Hollis stepped in front of her and said, "Barb, it's bad."

Barb made no reply. She sidestepped Hollis and hurried to the cabin. One step inside the door way, she froze. Her heart sank. She had not been prepared for the scene before her. Barb did not think anyone or anything could have prepared her for what she saw.

Barb saw Denny Smith and a woman she did not know

standing close together. Brock McGowen leaned on a pair of crutches staring at the floor. Barb's strong, vibrant husband lay on the deck covered in blood. He wore only a pair of cutoffs. Barb saw blood soaking the bandages that had been applied. Walter Ulrich kneeled beside her husband and wiped the blood from his face with a towel. Art was normally such an outgoing, healthy man that Barb thought the sight of him in this condition would kill her.

She instantly began to cry and gasped, "Oh, Art." Then, she rushed to his side. Blood was everywhere, on the floor, in Art's hair. Walt knelt in blood and it covered his arms up to his elbows.

Barb slipped her arms around her husband. She began to speak to him in a soothing voice, "Art, Art I'm here baby." She kissed his forehead and continued speaking, "It's all right. I love you Art."

Lynne Meyers had been a tomboy her entire life. She made a living in a man's world by being tough. However, this proved to be too much for her. She buried her head in Denny's chest and began to sob uncontrollably. Denny led Lynn from the cabin out to the stern deck arm in arm. Lynn could not stop sobbing. As they shuffled out of the cabin, she felt Denny's tears dropping onto her head.

Barb continued to speak in low, soothing tones. Art opened his eyes slowly and stared directly into her eyes. Barb knew he saw her.

Art's blue eyes sparkled for an instant and he managed a weak smile. His wish had come true. He saw his wife one more time. Then, Art Kendall let out a weak gasp and died.

"Noooooo!" Barb moaned. "Art, no, please don't leave me Art."

Brock limped out of the cabin. He made no attempt to hide the tears streaming down his face. Walt had not felt right since he took the hit on the head. He rose to his feet and stumbled out on deck. Feeling sick, he leaned on the gunwale and threw up over the side.

***

Twenty minutes later, as the pilot of the Coast Guard Jayhawk helicopter hovered the craft a hundred feet above the ocean. The co-pilot looked down. He had a good view. He saw three boats, a yacht, an R.I.B. and a workboat. The co-pilot watched his fellow service members from the Coast Guard as they took the occupants of the yacht into custody. He also saw five people on the deck of the workboat. He saw a man on crutches staring out at nothing. A thin man sat on the deck with his head in his hands. A blond-haired man embraced a woman and another man leaned over the side. This man wore only swim trunks and had broad shoulders. From this distance, the co-pilot could see the man did not look well. The co-pilot had a good view, but he could not see everything. If he could have seen inside the cabin of the workboat, he would have seen a woman holding her husband and quietly weeping.

Chapter Twenty-Two

Doctor Qeuokas eased his car out of the Route 1 traffic and onto Hibiscus Street in downtown Miami. The mid-morning traffic was light. He parked the Mercedes S-class sedan along the curb in front of a beige colored stucco office building. "I'll only be a minute," he told his wife. "I have some minor things to wrap up and we will be on our way."

The previous evening, he landed the floatplane and tied off at his private dock seven miles to the north. In the fading evening light, he unloaded the plane and drove to their downtown condominium.

The Doctor stepped out of the Mercedes and walked to the door of his practice. Just as he inserted the key in the door, two men from the U.S. Marshall Service appeared by his side.

As one man held her husband by the arm, Mrs. Qeuokas heard the other man begin to read out the Miranda Rights. A woman in a dark pantsuit rapped on the car window startling Mrs. Qeonnes. They had come for her and her husband. The Doctor's wife showed no emotion as the woman opened the car door and asked her to step out.

The Hurricane turned northeast and eventually blew itself out along the eastern coast of the U.S. causing minimal damage. Maria disappeared along with the silver she had taken. The same went for Bonita. Brock's fingers and one toe were gone, but he healed nicely. After four reconstructive surgeries, he recovered fully and walked with merely a slight limp. Walt had suffered a concussion, but had no long lasting issues.

The death of Art Kendall and the massive turnout at his funeral dominated the headlines in local and national news. From politicians and business magnates to laid-back surfers and adventurers a wide array of people paid their respects. On a dreary, drizzly day in North Carolina, Art was laid to rest.

Eight months later, Barb strolled gracefully along the plaza outside the Atlantis Hotel on Paradise Island in the Bahamas. She was there attending the wedding of Denny and Lynn. "Mr. and Mrs. Smith," Barb said approaching the newlyweds, "congratulations, what a beautiful wedding." She hugged both Lynn and Denny. She also hugged Brock who stood off to one side.

"I'm going to see what kind of beer they serve at this two-bit joint," Brock said. As he started to walk away, he added, "Don't forget Barb, you promised to save a dance for me."

Barb smiled and said, "My pleasure Brock. I'll see you later."

"Thank you for coming Barb," Lynn said.

"Yea, it means a lot to us," Denny added.

"I wouldn't miss it for the world. Kendall Outdoors has a few trips coming up. I'm looking forward to booking your air charter services."

"You'll get top notch service Barb, you can count on that," Denny said.

Barb said, "I'd better, or I'll go over your head to the boss." She gave Lynn a wink.

After Art's death, Walt, Brock, Denny, Lynn, and Hollis hired a commercial salvage crew to recover the remaining treasure. The find of the *Santa Luala* was one of the richest in history. The extensive expenses were paid in full. After paying the salvage crew a hefty fee, they split up the remainder. Maria, the little Cuban girl received a 50% share right off the top. They divided the rest of the find six ways. Despite his protests, they took Hollis on as a full partner. Walt argued and the rest agreed that after what he went through with them, he should be included as one of them. Each person cleared approximately 4.4 million dollars. Another 6 to 8 million in treasure waited to go through the cleaning process and then go up for sale.

Hollis did not change much. However, his fishing lure

collection received a healthy bump. He forged ahead with his contracting business.

Denny and Lynn used their money to start an air charter service. The business gave Denny the opportunity to fly on a regular basis. Lynn helped run the business and continued to Captain fishing charters when time allowed. For Denny and Lynn, a fulfilling life doing what they loved was now a bigger aspect than making money.

Barb created a foundation for Cuban refugees in Art's name with the entire amount of her cut. Brock retired and had not done much of anything for eight months. Walt planned to take a trip to the South Pacific. Meanwhile, he continued to work at his regular job.

"Has anyone seen Walt?" Barb asked.

Denny answered, "He walked down to the beach."

"I'm going to go say hi. Congratulations again. You two make a great couple."

She found Walt sitting on a wooden deck chair in the sand. The incongruous sight of a man dressed in a tuxedo on the beach brought a smile to her face as she padded through the soft white sand. Barb dropped into an empty chair beside him and said, "Hi Walt. Good to see you."

Walt had not noticed Barb's presence. He sat up straight and said, "Hello Barb, how are you?"

"I'm good," Barb said, nodding. After an awkward pause, she went on, "Life goes on Walt. I hear you're still working ... what are you waiting for? You have money now ... freedom. Get out there and enjoy your life."

Walt answered in a monotone voice, "I'm planning to hang it up in a few months. I'm going to take a trip to the South Pacific."

Barb sighed. After a brief pause she said, "It wasn't your fault. Art died the way he lived. He was always a man of honor, a hero."

"If I hadn't called ... "

"If you hadn't called," Barb interrupted, "you would have all died." They stared out at the turquoise ocean in silence for a long while before Barb said, "What would Art do? That's what I always ask myself. I was left with the business and a million and one decisions. Thousands of employees depend on me. Whenever I need strength, I ask myself, what would Art do?" Barb rose to leave. "Time to move on Walt. Take that trip. I'll expect photos from Tahiti, and you'd better be smiling."

This brought a slight grin to Walt's face.

"Actually," Barb said, "I have a proposition for you."

Walt felt his interest perk up. "A proposition?"

"Yes. Not long before Art died, he started a new television channel. The channel is called Seven Seas. Seven Seas is going to cover all aspects of the oceans from surfing and life on tropical beaches to life miles below the surface. Like twenty-four-hour news channels, Seven Seas will be twenty-four-hour coverage of events in and around the world's oceans."

"Sounds like a great idea."

Barb nodded, "Important issues will come to light and I think it will go over good with ratings."

"It doesn't surprise me that Kendall Outdoors would bring a top-notch product such as this to the table."

"The thing is," Barb said, "I need someone to produce the show."

Walt stared at her.

"I think you'd be a great choice."

"You have to be joking," Walt said.

"You're a leader. You're good on the ocean. You have that certain something ... I can't quite explain it, but I know you'd succeed."

"I'm flattered Barb, but I'm not a producer."

"I already have an executive producer to take care of most of the white-collar stuff. I need someone out in the field. Or, in this case, out on the oceans."

Walt was flabbergasted. "I don't know what to say."

"You don't have to answer now. We're at a wedding, a celebration. Enjoy yourself my friend. When you get back home and have some time, think about it. You could take your trip to the South Pacific first and start when you get back if you want. Or, on second thoughts, you could make it a working vacation ... go on the company's dime. Your trip could be the start of your career."

As Barb walked away, she looked back over her shoulder and said, "It won't be all fun and games you know. The ocean can be full of perils, but remember, you have to die of something."

A look of astonishment came over Walt's face. "What

did you say?"

Barb spun around to face Walt, but she kept backpedaling as she called, "Oh yes, you probably didn't know but I've heard Art say that dozens of times. 'Like my old buddy, Walt says, you gotta die of something.' Barb flashed a wave and a smile, turned, and continued walking.

Walt took a pen and a small notebook from a breast pocket in his tuxedo. He quickly wrote down his home phone number, cell phone and e-mail numbers. Catching up to Barb, he held out the piece of paper. Looking her straight in the eye, Walt said, "Barb Kendall, if you ever find yourself in trouble anywhere in the world, call and I'll be on my way."

Walt was serious and Barb understood. The realization of knowing men who say what they mean and mean what they say, and, who would risk their lives to help a friend brought a tear to the corner of her eye. Barb gave Walt a light kiss on the cheek and breathed, "Thank you."

"You're welcome Barb."

Brushing the tear from her eye, Barb straightened herself and said, "Well, I have to be going. I'm going parasailing this evening with some college girls I met on the flight from Miami, and I promised Brock a Polka before I leave."

"Polka! You know how to Polka?" Walt said, laughing.

"No, but who cares, it'll be fun. See you around, Walt, take care of yourself and let me know what you decide."

"So long, Barb."

Walt watched Barb walk away. After she left, he stared out at the tranquil water of the Caribbean with a smile and said aloud, "Get ready world, here I come."

THE END

About the Author

Keith Dissinger was born and raised the United States. He currently lives with his wife Anne in Western Canada where he works in the oil fields and writes Adventure novels.

To learn more visit Keith on his website

www.keithdissinger.com

Thank you for reading my book I truly appreciate it.

My next book is called **Hotel California** and will be released around the first week of March.

Here is a short sample of the opening of the book,

Hotel California

1

Even the two-hundred dollar Gucci sunglasses couldn't keep Sammy from squinting. He took a break from rolling his cigarette, laid his head back in the chair and admired his surroundings. Bright white sunlight shimmered on the otherwise deep blue Sea of Cortez.

He could see but not hear the waves breaking on the beaches of Cabo San Lucas half a mile away. A little farther inland, heat waves shimmered up from the hot Mexican desert. The only sounds he heard this far from land were the gentle waves lapping at the hull of the boat and the occasional squawk of a gull.

Sammy loved this area of the Baja peninsula and the freedom it provided from the hectic pace of Hollywood. He was considered an A-list Celebrity and a genuine movie star. Money wasn't a problem, but time and privacy were precious commodities for Sammy Sampson.

"Are we going to smoke some dope or what?" Lindsay's sing song voice brought him back from day dreaming.

Sammy eyed his current girlfriend. Lindsay Robbard's blond hair shone bright, almost white in the strong afternoon sun. She wore no top, only the tiniest thong bikini bottoms and as she stretched back in her lounge chair, Sammy noticed that her tan had darkened considerably in the last three days. Even the pale strips where her bikini straps normally crossed her shoulders and back were filling in. With her amazingly white teeth, long blond hair and perfectly proportioned body, Lindsay represented the true California girl and she looked right at home next to Sammy aboard his yacht aptly named Actor.

The Actor was a one-hundred and one foot luxury yacht. With a crew of five, she cost a small fortune to maintain, but Sammy made two movies a year for the past five years and at twenty million dollars a movie, there wasn't much he could not afford.

At thirty years of age, Sammy guessed he'd have many, many more years of making films and money before he was considered washed up. Famous actors were working well into their later years these days. However, he grew tired of filming. Crazy fans, promotional tours, and the whole famous

actor, Hollywood scene in general was burning him out. He craved privacy more than anything these days.

Sammy gazed at the after deck of the Actor. Kicked back in a lounge chair, Lindsay held a margarita in one hand and a Marlboro cigarette in the other. Curls of blue smoke drifted up from the cigarette. The surreal scene provided stunning portrait of Lindsay in front of the Cabo San Lucas back drop. Sammy imagined the crew was getting a good look at his topless girlfriend, but he didn't care, and if Lindsay cared, she sure did not show it. Sammy knew Lindsay was more interested in the lifestyle than in him. She enjoyed the fame, the shopping, and the expensive clothing and cars. She stayed with Sammy more for the coke, pot, alcohol, and expensive dinners than just being interested in him. He didn't mind. He used her, she used him. It sounded like a song, but in this life, everyone used everyone.

On the small, square table in between the lounge chairs there was a pitcher of lime margaritas, a bottle of suntan lotion, a pack of Marlboro, and a bag of excellent Mexican pot purchased in Cabo San Lucas the previous day. This was what Sammy lived for. In a few days, some of his Hollywood friends would join him on the yacht and then the real party would begin.

"Well?" Lindsay asked.

"Keep your pants on," Sammy replied. "Or don't on second thought."

"Shut up," Lindsay playfully replied before downing her drink in one long swallow. She licked the salt off the rim of the glass and stared at Sammy with tempting eyes.

Sammy finished rolling the joint and passed it to Lindsay. She lit it, took a long draw and handed it back. Sammy inhaled deeply and then rested his head on the lounger. He exhaled and watched the grey smoke spiral towards the cloudless blue sky. "This is what life's all about," said Sammy more to himself than to Lindsay. "This is it."

They smoked and drank the afternoon away rocking on the slow rolling indigo blue swells of the warm Mexican ocean. When the sun lowered in the western sky, they retired to the master state room for a quick nap and a shower.

Just as the fire-red sun sank below the horizon, Sammy and Lindsay returned to the rear deck. During the couple's absence, the crew transformed the rear deck of the Actor into an intimate setting.

A white table cloth covered a table set for two standing in the center of the deck. On the table, a candle flickered in the slight evening breeze. Warm lighting and soft music completed the scene. Sammy and Lindsay dined on Chicken Enchiladas with Pimento Cheese Sauce. Of course, large quantities of alcohol were consumed before and during the meal. Sammy rolled another joint after dinner.

Lindsay sat close to Sammy on the deck with her back against the gunwale. They smoked and drank while watching the moon rise over the low mountains along the Baja coast line. The almost full moon cast bright light and dark shadows over the mountain range. By eleven o'clock they were both passed out.

Alfy Mendez allowed himself a mere few seconds to stare at Lindsay Robbard. She now wore a sheer, lime green evening dress, but he'd seen her earlier in the day wearing far less. Even now as she lay passed out beside Mr. Sampson, he could easily imagine her body under the evening gown. Along with his eyes roaming over Lindsay's body, Alfy also took a few seconds to express his feelings for Sammy. "Sammy Sampson," he lamented in a hushed tone. "You have everything; money, health, women, and still you throw it all away."

Sammy and Alfy were the same age. While Sammy measured his income in the millions, Alfy made just enough to get by. However, he would not allow himself to dwell on his station in life. One of five children, he felt lucky and thankful that his single mother had the courage to immigrate to the U.S. when he was small and provide him with the opportunity for a decent life. He knew also that with no secondary education, in today's economy he was very fortunate to have this job. One day, he reasoned, he will have the home and family he had always wanted. And when he does, his wife will be a good woman, not cheap like Sammy's girl. He put these thoughts aside for it was time to get back to work. The evening temperature had cooled considerably. Alfy unfolded a large Mexican blanket and spread it out over the sleeping couple. They never stirred.

Alfy finished cleaning up the remains of dinner. He had just started for the main cabin when he heard a muffled thud against the hull near the stern of the Actor. When he reached the gunwale and peered over the side, he found himself staring directly into the face of a menacing man pointing a gun straight at his head.